KRISHNA

IN HIS LAST DAYS

DR. ASHOK SHARMA

M.Sc., Proficiency in French
Ph.D., (Maths)

redgrab books

Krishna: In His Last Days (Novel)
© Dr. Ashok Sharma

Price in india   : ₹ 150
Price out side india : $ 8

Published By : Redgrab books
                942, Mutthiganj, Allahabad, 211003
                website : anjumanpublication.com
                E-mail : contact@anjumanpublication.com

Printed at   : Repro Knowledgecast Ltd, Thane
Edition   : First, 2013
                  Second, 2017
ISBN   : 978-93-87390-05-8

To my parents

Late Siya Rani Sharma

Late Prem Shanker Sharma

Content

DR. ASHOK SHARMA

About The Author

Dr. Ashok Sharma, retired from Central Bank of India is known for his writings with historical and my mythological characters in centre. His previous publications 'Krishna: Antim Dino Mein', 'Seeta Sochtee Theen......' and 'Sita Ke Jane Ke Baad Ram' are known for his factual approach and excellent composition of characters.

His two collections of poems 'Shri Krishna Sharnam' and 'Mere Pankh Mera Aakash' are also published.

The speciality of his writing is that he never compromises with the pride and glory of any mythological character yet maintaining very interesting and readable nature of the book.

The modern trend of writings in Hindi and English literature is known as 'stream of consciousness'. Dr. Ashok Sharma has conscientiously linked himself with this school as his writings reveal.

The Submission

God had incarnated in the form of Krishna in Dwaper era, for repression of wicked ones and for redemption of good people. Deoki; the daughter of Devak and Vasudeo; the son of the king Shoorsen were his parents.

When the idea of writing on his last days came to my mind, several questions arose. What would have been the sentiments and the behaviour of Lord Krishna, when the thought of leaving this body had come to his mind? How would have he left? It did not seem easy to picture.

Then one more idea struck that if I am able to keep him in my heart and his picture in my eyes, it will be easier. There is a Shakti Peeth with a big temple of goddess Chandirka at Bakshi-Ka-Talab in Lucknow, U.P., where Barbareek; the grand-son of Bhim (one of the Pandvas) had worshipped God, with austere devotion.

I brought a small picture of Krishna from there and

placed it in front of me on my writing table. During the course of writing this book, there were many emotional experiences and sometimes I felt that I am really viewing that part of time. It can be called a feeling of bliss.

After writing a few pages it appeared that the stories of stealing of clothes of Gopis (the cow-maids) while they were taking bath in the river Yamuna and his having sixteen thousand one hundred wives are not in conformity with the character of Yogeshwer Bhagwan Krishna; the preacher of Bhagwad Geeta.

Later the stories of Draupdi living with five husbands, the accreditations about the birth of Dhirtrashtra, Pandu, Vidur, Karna and the five Pandavas appeared as simply an attempt of character-assassination of the women-folk, so it came to me that there should be reviewing of consideration.

This reviewing appeared to be more important because if the epics of Ram and Krishna are emitted from the history considering them as myth or the poet's fancy, the residual will be anything but not Bharat and it will be a great loss to human-civilization also.

Any attempt to add some imaginary incidents with uncultured and indecent contexts in these epics, to give some imaginative references to prove them true or some burdened philosophical explanations in their support is nothing, but a clear offence, but in vanity against the gravity, dignity and the glory of these characters.

It appeared to me that there was no systematised and orderly writing of history in that period of time. The history was being kept alive in the narrative ways in the religious discourses and hence the addition of some imaginative, illogical and interesting incidents and to give the entire episode a turn according to one's own liking, was easy and quite natural.

It should also be kept in mind that foreign invaders had destroyed our literature mercilessly. The Universities of Takchhshila and Nalanda are the burning examples of it, where the very rich and huge libraries were turned to ashes.

Since it was not possible for me to collect and verify all the facts, I took the help and references from the abridged Mahabharata of the Geeta Press, Gorakhpur and 'Purna Purushottam Bhagwan Shree Krishna'; the book written by Shrimad A. C. Bhaktivedant Swami Prabhupad, who resounded 'Hare Rama Hare Krishna' in many countries.

The entire Hindu society and not only the writer of these lines, will remain indebted to Maharshi Vyas who narrated the entire episode of Mahabharata otherwise these great characters would have been lost with the passage of time.

After Maharshi Vyas, it became a tradition to call Vyas, every one occupying that seat at different intervals of time. Naturally, they too, would have added or deleted some contexts, but such stories are very far from the logic and confined up to the sentiments and the sense of reverence. Such stories are found very often in the religious books and discourses of almost every cult.

I have tried to make a logical analysis of such stories regarding Krishna and the women-characters of that epic which appeared me thrust on these characters by fantastic imaginations, baseless, cooked and publicised with a special bent of mind.

These characters have been so distorted that no one wants to name a girl Draupadi, in his family, not even the persons who express reverence to her and say that having five husbands at a time was in conformity with our scriptures. The contexts of Draupadi are so spread in Mahabharata as if Draupadi was the leading character, next only to Krishna.

The doubt that these contexts are not based on facts but are cooked one, strengthens when Draupadi's conversations with these so called husbands, e.g. chapters like Yudhishthir-Draupadi Samvad, Arjun-Draupadi Samvad, Bhim-Draupadi Samvad are so detailed and spread in so many pages as if the person writing these stories was sitting in between them.

A person can describe the events around him, but how one can give the details of a personal conversation between a husband and his wife. It indicates that this is not an exact description, but the work of a fertile mind.

It may be true that Maharshi Vyas was blessed with divine insight but this assumption that he was over-hearing and writing the details of a personal conversation between a wife and a husband is a derogatory remark on him. It is said that he had written the book "Jai" which with so many additions became Mahabharata. It can be said to be its distortion.

To say an untruth repeatedly and in different styles depicts it as a truth. In many cases the events appear to be purposefully planted and manifestation of an ill-will.

Be it, the book Geet Govindam of Jai Deo or the degraded writings giving body details of these revered characters or the mockeries on the stages, are examples of crooked intelligence and put a question mark on the mind-set of such people.

Some scholars may call this attempt of analysing these stories wrong and offensive, but after reading this book, it may appear to them and many others a right approach, enlarging the stature of these characters and I have written this book with this belief and intention in my mind.

Today, the people of new generation have no time even if they have interest, to read these old and voluminous books. This book is an attempt to convey that literature to them in an interesting and brief way with logical considerations.

While writing this book I have tried, with his picture on my table to keep Bhagwan Shree Krishna in my heart and my strong belief is that it was his inspiration that I could write this book. SO IF THERE IS ANY THING WORTH AND APPRECIABLE IN IT, IT IS HIS; THE LORD, BUT ALL THE LACKS AND LAPSES ARE MINE.

I have tried my best to reach at logical conclusions and make this book interesting and acceptable to the new generation also. I have given an epilogue at the end of the book to prove the historicity of Lord Krishna and Mahabharata. I feel indebted to my literary friend and a very senior litterateur Shri Shiv Narayan Mishra, Gosainganj, Lucknow for giving valuable suggestions in shaping this book.

- Ashok Sharma

1.

Memories Around

Krishna was sitting on a rock on the sea-shore of Dwarika thoughtful, calm and alone. Major part of his life, right from Kansa-vadh was spent in fights and wars. Now, when all of this had ended, he once again remembered the magical music of the flute, he used to play in his childhood.

The enchanting notes of this flute moved in rhythm to the entire Gokul and Vrindavan and drew Radha from the village Barsana to Vrindavan to listen to that music.

Sometimes Radha, hiding this flute, made Krishna dance to her tunes. The elixir of life rained in those happy and rhythmic moments full of divinity of love. He was only around eleven years of age when Akroor had taken him to Mathura and after that he could never come back to Gokul.

Krishna raising his eyes looked at the sea and the sky

meeting on the horizon. The sky in the west was red. The rays of the sun had come a long way and were playing with the waves of the sea.

A few birds and some small fishes had also joined the play. Very often some fast moving waves of the sea drenched the feet of Krishna. The noise of the waves was increasing with the evening passing off gently.

The eyes of Krishna were on the horizon but his heart was somewhere else. The memories of Gokul and Vrindavan had filled his heart and the events shared with Radha were flashing in his mind. Once Radha had taken the flute from him and had said,

"I will not return it to you. It always rests on your lips and it hurts me somewhere. If its sound is so dear to you, let me play it and you listen."

Even a defeat in those discussions was a delight. Krishna took the flute out of his clothes, put it on his lips, closed his eyes and started playing it. The flute strutted on its fate. It was on the lips of Krishna, a place which was soft, beautiful, pink and pious. Even Sudarshan Chakra which always remained on the forefinger of his right hand could only envy it.

Suddenly a small fish touched his feet along with sea water. Krishna felt it and looked at his feet. He used to stand cross-legged while playing the flute among his childhood friends. Once Lalita, a very intimate to Radha had said,

"Look, think twice before giving Krishna, a place in your heart because once he is in, he will cross his feet as usual and will never leave."

Radha with redness on her face, had replied,

"Yes, I know that."

The very remembrance of this incident filled his heart with sentiments. He started walking on the sand alongside the sea, in a contemplative mood. The marks of his feet left on the sand were deep and clear like those left by him on the canvas of time.

He once again came to the rock and sat on it. The evening was passing out. The rays of the sun were shrinking in the sky. A few leaves fallen from the trees were floating on the wind. Krishna felt, the entire life blows on the wings of time in the same fashion.

The construction work of Dwarika, surrounded by strong walls covering an area of approximately ninety six square miles was complete. It was well designed by Vishwakarma; a well known architect and engineer. It had planned roads, trees and a number of great mansions.

The people living in Dwarika were happy and prosperous. Kalyavan had already died at the hands of Muchkund; the son of king Mandhata; a descendent of lord Ram belonging to Ichhwaku Dynasty. The transfer of willing people of Gokul and the nearby areas to Dwarika was also almost complete.

His mind was busy in contemplation. Giving a bird`s eye view to the events starting from his incarnation on this earth, it appeared to him that the very purpose of this human body was accomplished and now, it was time to leave. Suddenly he remembered that in his previous birth he had killed Bali by shooting an arrow at him. At that time he had hidden himself behind a tree.

Krishna felt that his debt is still on him. Bali had taken birth as Jara, a fowler. He decided that this time Jara will deceitfully shoot an arrow at him and he will leave this body. This way of leaving the body appeared him human and an appropriate repayment of that debt.

Once reaching on the decision to leave, the memories of his childhood again flashed his mind. In the dawn of the day, he used to touch the feet of his fostering parents Nand and Yashoda whom he used to call Baba and Maan. His days always started with their blessings. He used to go to a nearby temple after his mother gave him a bath. Then he was given milk and fruit in breakfast by his mother.

Various mischief of childhood struck his mind. His mother used to prepare curd and butter from milk putting hard labour but Krishna very mischievously and secretly used to distribute it among his friends. Sometimes the earthen container was broken in this game. Normally the mother used to laugh at his naughty acts but very often, it perturbed her.

Once, his mother tied him with a mortar as a punishment. Krishna tried to break the rope tying him, by dragging the mortar between two trees. The trees were uprooted in this process. His mother Yashoda knew that her son was an extra-ordinary child. She laughed at it but felt proud of him.

There were so many pea-cocks in those days. Although his mother rebuked him for his mischief but looking to the might of her son, she picked-up a feather of peacock, put it on his forehead decorating his hair, put her hand on his head, caressed, kissed him and said,

"Krishna, always remain a sense of delight for good people but at the same time a regent of death for the evil ones."

Since then he always used to put a feather of peacock in his hair as a part of his coronet. This always remained a source of inspiration to him for welfare of the good people and repression of the evil ones.

A sentimental mood surrounded him. He looked at his clothes and one more event related to his fostering mother Yashoda came to his mind.

It was Basant Panchmi; a festival celebrated to mark the arrival of spring season. People worship Saraswati; the goddess of knowledge and wisdom and wear yellow clothes on this day. There was a huge gathering at his house to celebrate this day. It was like giving a grand welcome to the spring season. After Sarsvati-Pujan people started greeting one another and started enjoying the occasion.

The atmosphere was full of fun and merriment. The moments were marvellously joyful. Men and women were dancing and playing musical instruments. A few women who were close to Yashoda wanted her to join them but due to the presence of Nand, blushing Yashoda refused to participate. One of them who was very intimate to Yashoda said,

"Yashoda, are you not feeling pleasure on the arrival of the spring?"

At that time little Krishna was near his mother and he could never forget the reply given by his mother to that lady. She had said,

"The spring comes only once in a year for you but since Krishna has come in my life, every day is full of spring for me. This is why I always dress-up him in yellow clothes."

After this reply she took Krishna in his lap and said,

"Look, my spring season is always in my lap."

Krishna grew older, went away from his mother Yashoda, Baba Nand and his town Gokul but he could never forget that incident and gave too much importance to the yellow clothes, so that his mother could have a feel of spring throughout the year. As a result, many people started calling him Pitamberdhari; a person in yellow clothes.

The sea winds were gaining speed and sound of their crossing over the big trees and that of waves of sea was increasing. Krishna rose from the rock, went to stand under a tree, looked at his yellow cloths, put one foot across the other, took the flute out of his clothes, put it on his lips, closed his eyes and started playing it.

The memories of Vrindavan filled his eyes. Lost in the melodious sound of the flute, a few moments past, he felt a touch as soft as feather on his hand. The touch appeared to be a known one. He opened his eyes saying, 'Radha', but to his utter surprise, he found a leaf from the tree had come to rest on his hand. He smiled.

Someone touched

In a way

As if it was nothing

But only the winds

And the illusion.

The sky was becoming darker. The sun had almost immersed in the sea, only a few red rays rising from the place of immersion of the sun in the sea had taken the challenge of spreading light. Krishna, lost in memories, lips a little screwed but smiling, started moving slowly towards his palace. As he entered, attendants approached him for instructions if any, but he entered his room without noticing them. Rukmini, who was waiting, came hurriedly.

She was worried and impatient. The seriousness on the face of Krishna perturbed her and when he sat Rukmini also took a seat beside him and looked at his face.

"Are you worried?" She asked.

Krishna smiled, took the flute out of his clothes, put it aside, caressed Rukmini moving his hand on her head to normalise her and then properly placing locks fallen on her forehead, said,

"No, Rukmini, I am not."

"Look, I am your wife and know you well. Your face is telling that definitely there is some cause of worry.

Krishna took hold of her hands, laughed and looking at her face, said,

"Rukmini you are unnecessarily worried, there is nothing like that.

Krishna could not open his heart. His statement silenced Rukmini, but with apprehensions. She looked at his face and felt helpless.

With the sky in the eyes

A feeling of someone beyond boundaries

And a sense of own limitations

Filled her heart.

It was time for dinner. An attendant came to them. Krishna rose, reached dining-hall and took a seat. Rukmini her-self served the dinner and took a seat beside him. Krishna asked her to join but she said politely,

-"You do. I will take my dinner later."

Krishna silently took the dinner, Rukmini kept watching intently at his face with affinity and satisfaction. Krishna finished but some eatables were left in his plate. Rukmini took the same plate for herself. Krishna checked,

"Why don`t you take a fresh plate? You should take care of yourself also."

"With all considerations for my-self, to take food in these pots is both my right and fortune," she said.

"Please finish your dinner and then we will go for a walk." He said and added after a pause,

"Rukmini, you are immensely good and my great fortune."

Rukmini listened but said nothing. She was perturbed due to serious and worried posture of Krishna. He had taken meal for the name sake and it had further intensified her grief. This affectionate behaviour of Krishna filled her eyes. She took a little food and washed her hands.

Krishna realised her pain, wiped her tears, helped her hand and came out of the walls. There were plants and trees around, winds blowing with fragrance of Jasmine and moon and some scattered stars in the clear sky.

Krishna with Rukmini took seat on a little higher place with one foot on the earth and the other skewed and resting on it. Rukmini fixed eyes on them.

There were yellow clothes, bluish feet and pinkish nails and soles. The pink colour of soles was rising a little up on his feet. Rukmini became sentimental staring at them. She prayed,

"O god, let these feet be always with me and never depart."

With the sky in the eyes
Breathings lost in the air
The sense of own-self disappeared
Like a drop of water in the vast ocean.

Krishna who was looking at the moon turned his eyes, looked at Rukmini, took hold of her hands and started looking in the void. The old memories had revived.

* * *

Rukmini was the only daughter of Maharaja Bhishmak having five brothers, a flawless beauty, very learned one and brought-up with royal splendour. Great saints like Narad used to visit the royal court of Bhishmak.

Rukmini had heard about Krishna from them and was nursing a desire to have him as her life-partner but her elder brother Rukmee had decided to marry her with Shishupal, the son of king Damghosh. Maharaja Bhishmak had accepted it only because Rukmee was his eldest son and hence the heir of the throne, but he him-self was very much impressed with Krishna and was therefore not very enthusiastic about that relationship.

Rukmini sent a letter to Krishna at Dwarika through a messenger. The scenes thereafter, flashed in Krishna's mind. Before her swayamwar (an ancient culture wherein a bride chooses her husband on her own amongst a number of aspirants assembled at one place) Rukmini had gone to worship goddess Durga and while on the way back from the temple, Krishna with a chariot of four horses reached there.

The chariot, it was having a flag with the figure of a hawk. Although it was a huge crowd Rukmini did no mistake in recognising him. She moved towards that chariot and Krishna helped her to ride it holding her hand and then with Rukmini on it, the chariot sped up.

Shishupal and other kings calmed down after expressing their anguish but Rukmee challenged and chased them. After a short fight Krishna defeated Rukmee depriving him of his chariot and weapons.

Krishna wanted to give death penalty to him but he was the brother of Rukmini and she was very much aggrieved imagining a harsh punishment to him. With a faded face and tears in her eyes, she looked at Krishna and uttered only one word, 'Pardon'.

Krishna stopped and let Rukmee go. Rukmini remained calm and lost during the entire journey. Many questions were haunting her mind. What would have been the reaction of her family members? The injuries Rukmee had sustained may be deep. How will he be well? She knew her bosom maids who knew about her love for Krishna will be happy, but will be panicky about the consequences of this entire episode.

Krishna was continuously trying to console her. Although she received a grand welcome at Dwarika, she could be normal only after her marriage with Krishna was ceremoniously performed with traditional rituals.

She had full faith in Krishna, but still there were worries in her mind. Memories of his parents were also striking her, but she was very much consoled when she found the parents of Krishna; Deoki and Vasudeo very affectionate to her from the very first day. Deoki had embraced her the very moment she met.

Just then the flow of thoughts in Krishna's mind stopped and he noticed that Rukmini was sitting with her eyes fixed on his feet. Krishna invited her attention,

"Rukmini," he called.

Rukmini looked at him with a faded smile on her face. Krishna asked,

"Rukmini, how much time would have passed?"

"It seems to be late at night. The calm around is deep but you appear to be embedded in thoughts. The expressions on your face are vocal. Definitely there is something in your mind. I feel that even after living so long with you I have not been able to reach your heart."

"No, please don't think so. You are always in my heart, but true, some past memories are haunting my mind. Rukmini see, I am so unfortunate a son that my parents were put in jail only on the apprehension of my birth. They were only a just married couple at that time. They remained in prison until I was grown up enough to give a death penalty to Kansa. They had to spend a major part of their youth in prison."

"That is right but how are you responsible for that? The destiny is also there and the persons like Kansa always discover one reason or the other to torture the good people. You had freed them from prison killing Kansa when you were just an adolescent. Today they are living happily in a grand palace with so many attendants. This has also been done by you," said Rukmini and then as if something more has come to her mind, she added,

"Do you somewhere feel that I am not taking their proper care and that is adding to your worries about them."

"No Rukmini, on the contrary, since your arrival you have not let them feel alone and they are always full of praise for you and that they were in prison is not a question of fixing responsibility, but I was the reason behind that, and it somewhere pains me. They spent all those days in prison enduring the atrocities of Kansa, for whom the people wait and whose recollection fills them with pleasure," he said and after a pause added,

"Look, my foster parents Yashoda and Nand had nurtured me with great love and care. Even my mischief was a pleasure for them, but the circumstances were such that I could never return to Gokul and serve them." And Krishna stopped, closing his eyes.

Rukmini saw his exhausted face, broad forehead, dark eyes and vocal lips. She put her palm soft like petals of a flower, on his forehead and arranged his hair with her fingers.

"Lord, I can understand your pain, but Kansa had imprisoned your parents due to a divine revelation forecasting his death at the hands of their son and you were not even born till then, so why do you feel guilty? Moreover no fortune can be a greater than getting a son like you.

Your foster parents Nand and Yashoda enjoyed your childhood and that too was no less a pleasure and fortune. It was greater than the return of all the good deeds put together. You could not give them time only due to your continuous engagements in the welfare of society and not due to any personal interest. You were not negligent to them, so why are you sad?"

The arguments of Rukmini affected Krishna. He, feeling relaxed looked at her face. It was full of the divine beauty shining in the moonlight, but apart from this there was splendour of a very learned person. A very pleasant feeling of getting Rukmini filled his heart.

Like a pot full of elixir

A flawless moon showering soft light

Came to hands

But a few drops spilled

And the fragrance emitting

Jasmine flowers smiled.

2.

Notes of Affection

Winds were gaining speed and it was moonlight spread all over. Tired and exhausted Rukmini was sleeping with her head resting on Krishna`s shoulder.

He was looking casually toward the sky and very often towards her face. The logics put forward by Rukmini had consoled him a lot, but the sleep was still away from his eyes.

Krishna, full of praise and gratitude looked towards her face. Rukmini`s hand was on his shoulders, but her face was tilted downwards.

He tried to raise her head to keep properly on his shoulder, but was startled. Lo, it was the face of Radha. Surprisingly he shook it. The lethargic face opened eyes. Yes, it was Radha. He asked,

"Oh, Radhey, how did you come?"

"I was never away. Did you not search your heart?"

"But Radhey, it was Rukmini here."

"Don`t try to find difference between Rukmini and me."

"But Rukmini is my wife."

"Yes, she is and I am not so, but marriage takes place between the two different people and we are not two. Can you think of any formal tie between one the same?"

"Agreed, but the appearance of your face in place of Rukmini is startling."

"Rukmini is guileless and it is your own image in her shining beauty."

"But it is you, Radhey."

"I repeat, please ask your own-self. We are always one and same."

It silenced Krishna. After a pause he said,

"Radhey, after leaving Gokul I was roaming between Mathura, Hastinapur, Kurukshetra, Indraprasth, Dwarika and so many other places. There were a number of battles, wars and so many other engagements. So I had at least some excuses for living away from you but Radhey how could you live without me."

"I have never lived without you. My part of Krishna was always with me."

"What are you saying Radhey? Is it possible to posses a person in parts?"

"Yes, possible, it is possible. Look, a child who played in the courtyard of Nand and Yashoda, played with cow-boys and cow-maids, tended cows and did fun and frolics, is their part of Krishna.

A person who fought battles and wars for victory of the truth at different places and lived his life as a loving husband is Rukmini`s part of Krishna, but the one playing flute and always living in my heart is my part of Krishna.”

After calm for a while, Radha added further,

“Uddhava had come, and was telling us that he had come on your behest but he was preaching us to forget you. Probably he did not know that you are stubborn in our hearts keeping your feet across.

Any suggestion to forget you was just like depriving us from our part of Krishna also. He was telling us to remember God and forget Krishna, look at the sun, but keep away from it's light.

It was just like an advice to keep body without soul. Still he was better than Akroor who had taken you to Mathura on a chariot at the age of eleven only.”

“But Radhey, that was necessary. My parents were in prison facing all the atrocities of Kansa. Also the kingdom of Mathura was to be returned back to Maharaja Ugrasen; the father of Kansa. Actually Kansa had dethroned his father and made him captive .There were certain other reasons also behind Akroor's act.”

“I know,” said she, then taking the left hand of Krishna in her hand, took hold of his little finger in her fist.

“Krishna, while in Gokul you had lifted the hillock Govardhan and that too, for a number of days on this finger alone. Your hands are too soft. How could you keep lifted that heavy hillock on it for so many days?” she asked.

Krishna did not reply, only smiled.

"I remember, your finger had turned dark red and remained so for a long time. There must have been immense pain. How could you bear with that?" she said.

This time Krishna laughed a little and said,

"Only you can keep in mind, my so small pains for such a long time, but the fact is that all the pains lose their existence before me."

"But Krishna, why the pain you have given to me is always alive."

"It is so because you don`t want to let it die. You want to keep it alive."

Krishna held the hand of Radha gently, pressed and touched it with his forehead. Radha shied but felt nice. She said,

"Krishna, I still remember it as an incident of last day only. Indra; the god of rain was angry and it was raining so heavily as if it would erase the entire Gokul. At that time it was you Krishna who kept us safe," and stopping for a while she further added,

"And Krishna, once, you had jumped from Kadamb tree on Kaliya Nag to teach him a lesson. I still shudder when I remember that incident. Your maan Yashoda had almost fainted and despite very strong belief in your valour, the entire Gokul and Vrindavan were sad and perturbed. Only your elder brother Balram was confident and smiling".

"That was only because he knew that this Krishna, wearing a peacock`s feather in the locks of his hair on his forehead, as a symbol of his mother`s blessings, is not afraid of any person, be it Kaliya Nag or any one else."

"Krishna, that wicked person Kaliya Nag belonging to the nag community was living on the banks of Yamuna with his family. He and his family members were so cruel and violent that people did not dare to go near those banks, but after that day he and his family members left that place for ever and the water of Yamuna became lifeline of the people living in the nearby suburbs."

"And Radhey, I never forget those moments of Vrindavan when I used to play the flute sitting under a tree in some grove and you listening to it, used to come almost running to that place.

That tune of flute mixed with the tinkling of your anklets created a wonderful musical sound.

The beauty of those moments can only be felt. That can not be described. Sometimes you came barefoot without bothering about the thorns in the way and I used to take those thorns out of your feet. The blood oozing out in this action hid in redness of your soles."

"Krishna, any one desirous of coming to you never bothers about the thorns in the way since he knows that you will take all the thorns off his feet but Krishna I would like to say one thing."

"Yes please do."

"Krishna, whenever I remember the touch of your fingers on my feet I am thrilled. It gives me a mixed feeling of guilt and the shyness.

"What are you saying Radhey? You yourself say that there is no difference between you and me, then what is wrong if I removed those thorns of your feet and why do you feel guilty for the same?"

"Because, if a woman does not have feelings of

respect for a person it becomes very difficult for her to love him and in my case it was one step ahead. I had the feelings of reverence for you.

So whenever you touched my feet this feeling of reverence for you gave me the feelings of guilt and the feeling of shyness is quite natural in such cases."

After this Radha stopped awhile, then said,

"Okay, now I am leaving."

Krishna, staring at her face could not say anything. The face of Radha faded out gradually and Krishna saw it was Rukmini sleeping with her head on his shoulder. Krishna raised her head gently and with a helping hand moved towards the palace with her.

Something,
As a fragrance from somewhere
Was in the air
One could not decide its origin
And lo, a buff came
Filled the body and the soul
But carried the fragrance away

3.

Sentiments Spilled

The Morning had come. Krishna awoke with the chirping of birds. Rukmini was already busy in the household chores. Krishna felt he is late in rising. He remembered it was Monday and Rukmini will not take water even, without worshipping in the nearby Shiv temple. He hurriedly got ready. Rukmini already was. Both went to the temple. While performing rituals and prayers she became sentimental. Tears welled up her eyes. Krishna wiped them with his cloth and asked,

"What has happened Rukmini? You are weeping."

"Please promise that you will never go away from me."

Coming out of the temple, Krishna held her hand and said,

"You are my strength Rukmini. None can separate us," and then in a jolly mood he added,

"Not even your brother, Rukmee."

"I am not bothered about Rukmee. He can not dare to look at us but I am full of apprehensions and since last evening very uneasy and restless."

"Please speak out those apprehensions. Has anybody annoyed you?"

"None can dare it till you are with me, but since last evening you appear as worried and uneasy, I can not take it casually and consequently there are apprehensions in my mind."

Krishna tried to laugh loudly,

"Rukmini, you are unnecessarily worried. Yesterday while sitting on the sea-sore for a long time I had got lost in some memories but when I realised that it is time to move home, I left for home and of course I was a little tired too."

While saying this, Krishna had in mind that he may not tell a lie. It was a time of return to his real home so he was not incorrect.

"And Rukmini, I promise not to leave you alone in my life."

Rukmini sensed some thing in this statement but could not say anything.

"Come with me. Let us go to Maan and Pitashri and take their blessings."

"Oh, you have spoken my words. Definitely it will be my pleasure."

Rukmini and Krishna reached the palace of Deoki and Vasudeo. Rukmini covered her head with sari. Both of them touched their feet and received blessings. Deoki embraced them. Vasudeo took hold of Krishna`s hand and seated him beside. It was the time of breakfast. There were fruit, milk and butter. Rukmini chopped fruit and served it to others but did not take it for her-self out of hitch. Deoki noticed it and affectionately said,

"Please join us Rukmini," and addressing Vasudeo she added,

"Our Krishna has brought a very good daughter-in-law for us."

"Maan, you please begin, I will take it later," Rukmini said.

"She is really very good. Her parents have taught her the real good values," Vasudeo added.

"You are correct. Her father is a virtuous and splendorous king and she has inherited virtues from her parents," Deoki said.

Rukmini`s face turned reddish. She said,

"Maan, The real fortunate person is me. All the happiness of the world has come to my aanchal (the extreme upper part of sari) by becoming your daughter-in-law."

Deoki turned the direction of the talks and said,

"Rukmini, we were not fortunate enough to enjoy the childhood of Krishna, but it is said that he was very naughty and although he has many achievements to his credit now, still he appears a child to me."

"Maan, I am always a child for you, this is true."

"Krishna, when we are talking about your childhood, please let me know one thing. Pootana was sent by Kansa to kill you and you were still a newly born child at that time. How could you know her motives and killed her?"

By now Krishna was very comfortable. The uneasiness of last night was over and he was feeling delighted in the company of his parents. Smilingly he said,

"Maan, I had not killed her."

This was something astonishing for Deoki, she countered,

"Then how did she die? Moreover I have heard that she got a place in heaven. Whether it was an appropriate reward for such an act?"

The delighted mood of Krishna had consoled Rukmini and she was feeling good.

"Maan, shall I tell you what he has told me about that incident," she said.

"Yes Rukmini, please," Deoki said.

"Maan, Pootana had not come on her own perspective. She was forced by Kansa for the same and she was bound to obey him otherwise Kansa would have delivered a very painful death to her. When she arrived, she found Gokul in a zealous, delighted and gaiety mood. It was only due to the birth of the child Krishna. She could never imagine of such an atmosphere in the kingdom of Kansa where people used to live in fear due to his atrocities.

Yashoda, the mother of the child put Krishna in her lap with trust and without wiles. The very purpose of her arrival shocked her intensely and when she saw his beautiful, innocent and smiling face, motherly affection for him filled her heart.

She had come with an evil intent but found her-self locked in his affection. It created an unbearable conflict in her heart. It trembled imagining the consequences, could not sustain and stopped.

That way Pootana was saved from performing a dreadful act but had paid with her life and consequently got a place in heaven."

Others had finished their breakfast. Rukmini served for her-self also, keeping her back towards her father-in-law. Krishna, although he was sitting with his own people but was again lost in memories of Radha. To him Radha`s love, sacrifice and dedication were incomparable.

How simply and spontaneously she had said that they are one and the same and hence the question of marriage between them does not exist, but definitely there would have been a lot of strife in her mind before saying so.

To become acquainted with Radha`s personality it is important to keep Krishna in background, just as a ray can be seen only when it is dark, he thought and then suddenly an event of past flashed in his mind.

He with Radha and her bondmaids was sitting in Vrindavan. A black bee came and started whirling around her face. Radha was startled. Her bondmaids asked Krishna to drive it off. Krishna only laughed but did not try for the same. After whirling awhile, the black bee went away. When Radha became normal she complained,

"Krishna, you did not drive it off. Why so?"

Krishna replied, "That was not needed."

"But it could harm me."

"No Radhey, it could not. It was attracted towards

your face under the illusion of a flower but it could never enter your aura. To tolerate your splendour was beyond its capabilities."

"Oh, leave it," Radha blushed. Her face had turned red on Krishna's this remark.

Just then Vasudeo called,

"Krishna."

The chain of thoughts was broken. Startled he replied,

"Yes,"

"Where are you?"

"Here only, but yes I had some thing in my mind which pains me very often.'

"And what is that?"

"Sometimes your sufferings due to me in the past strike my mind. Both of you were kept in jail just after your marriage and it was due to me, hence a sense of guilt is always there in my mind."

"Krishna, please don`t think so. Your mother and I my-self are very proud of you. You have left impressions on the canvas of time by your deeds. Their glory will never die and time will never forget us as well, for giving birth to a child like you. The sufferings of prison are very little before this pleasure."

"Pitashree, there is one more thing which haunts me badly. I was the reason behind the death of my seven brothers in their infancy."

"What is wrong with you Krishna? You are mistaken again. Those children had only that much of life. Being the part of a big design, it was Kansa and not you who had killed them. You are unnecessarily sorry for that. Have you forgotten your preaching to Arjun at the time of Mahabharat and feeling sorry for these perishable bodies?"

"No, I have not forgotten my words, but their essence was, that truth should never bother about any victory or defeat in a battle with untruth. I my-self have always fought for the destruction of evils but my innocent brothers were just infants when killed by Kansa. They were not in any fight. That was a condemnable and sad act. Naturally your agony must have been beyond imagination."

"Krishna, this type of nervous presentation on your part is demoralising and painful for us. You are dearer than life to us and will always remain so. I think that now this chapter should end for ever otherwise may be for the first time in life, but I will be displeased with you," said Deoki.

"Okay Maan, but this discussion has relieved me a lot."

Rukmini who was a silent listener up-till now, said,

"Maan, he is disturbed since last evening so it is good that he has conversed with you people on this subject. This definitely would have given him peace."

"Krishna, if you will feel disturbed on such petty matters how would you be able to help others?" Deoki said.

"Maan, you are correct and now there are no regrets in my heart."

"Krishna, let us go for a walk on the sea-side. It will be pleasant and relieving," Vasudeo said.

"Okay and I will drive the chariot. I am a good charioteer," said Krishna. He was in light mood, but Deoki took it seriously and added,

"Krishna, you are driving our chariot since beginning. Moreover at present we don`t want any third person among us."

All the persons took seat in the chariot and Krishna drove it to the sea-sore. In the way Deoki said,

"Krishna, I have one thing to say. You freed us from the shackles on your birth. Again with Akroor, you came to Mathura, freed us from the prison of Kansa. You have broken all our bondages. At present you are giving us the incomparable pleasures in Dwarika.

Now this is our last wish that please give us your heavenly abode, freeing from all the worldly bondages at the time of our departure from this world. We don`t want any rebirth and bondages again."

Rukmini also listened to it. She wondered and was speechless awhile, but later she said,

"Maan, what are you saying? What does it mean?"

"My son has understood what I mean."

Krishna was silent. He could not say anything, only took hold of his mother`s hand, pressed a little and this way gave a silent consent.

Rukmini looked at Deoki and then at Krishna, tried to read his face and said,

"I think, I too have understood."

She kept looking at his face. Her eyes were wet. Krishna was getting the accusation hidden in her eyes. Rukmini saving the eyes of his in-laws, said in a very low tone,

"Don`t forget me also."

* * *

The chariot reached the sea-shore; every one stepped down of it and together moved towards the sea. Krishna and Rukmini were behind the elders. Deoki and Vasudeo sat on the sand alongside the sea.

The winds were blowing and the sea-birds were flying and floating on the water. A few fish sparkled while leaping. Krishna and Rukmini waking along the sea-side went a little away looking at the oyster-shells lying on the sand. Krishna was again lost in some thoughts. Looking towards sky he said,

"Rukmini,"

Rukmini looked at him.

"Did I abduct you?" he said.

"No, on the contrary you saved me. You were my own selection. Had you been a little late in reaching there Rukmee would have definitely yoked me with the person like Shishupal."

"And when you had garlanded me as a token of your selection, was it not my duty to bring you here saving you from Rukmee, Shishupal and various other kings."

"Yes it was, but why are you raising these questions now?"

"Because Rukmee and Shishupal spread it mischievously that I had abducted you and it gives an impression that I am a slave of my senses."

"Whenever one tries to spit on the sun, it comes back to him only and the sun is never moved by it."

"You are correct Rukmini; it is worthless to talk on this subject. Don`t know why, but now-a-days something or the other of the past comes to my mind and disturbs me."

".If it is so then please promise that whenever any perturbing thing comes to your mind you will share it with me."

"Okay I will. Now let us go to our elders and sit with them for awhile."

"Right, probably they will be waiting for us and the biggest thing for me is that you will not be able to maintain this serious posture before them."

When they reached back to Deoki and Vasudeo, they were really waiting for them.

"Come, had you gone far away? The sun is becoming hot and we should get back," Vasudeo said. In their way back Deoki affectionately seated Rukmini beside her in the chariot.

4.

When the Pains Knocked

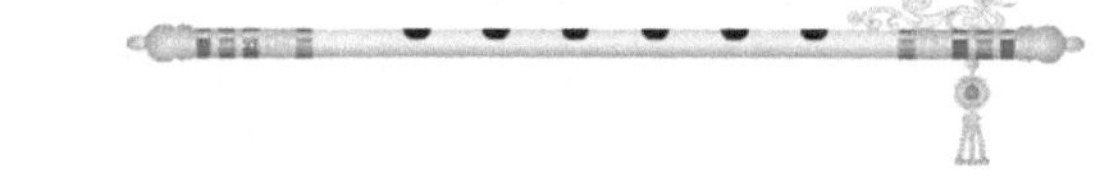

It was the evening. Krishna reached the roof of his palace slowly stepping up the stairs, came to balcony and looked around. There were far reaching rows of trees, some scattered houses, the sea beyond them and chorus of birds coming back to their roosts in the trees.

Krishna looked towards the sky. It was blue and clear, the sun setting in the west looked like a big red ball rolling down towards the sea.

The evening was peaceful and pleasant. Just then a little cool wind coming from east revived the memories of Vrindavan.

Winds from east always did so, but this time there was an aroma of the earth of that place with these winds. Whether it was an illusion? He was but sure, it can not be an illusion. He can never err in this matter. This aroma inhabits in his breaths.

Suddenly he felt someone has come flying with the wind and is standing beside him. He turned and found it was Radha. This time the surprise was not so big as it was when he had seen Radha's face in place of that of Rukmini. In a very natural tone he said,

"Radhey please come. When I had found aroma of Vrindavan in the air, I had concluded that it must have had the touch of your feet and you will definitely be somewhere around."

"Yesterday night, you were in gloomy mood and it is the same at present. This is something very unusual of you, so I could not stop my-self. Krishna, since our childhood I have never seen you sad. The Krishna of these days is somewhat different from the Krishna I know."

"Radhey these days I don't know why, but the memories of the past haunt me whenever they find me alone. Just now it was the memory of Kansa, my maternal uncle. He had made several attempts to get me killed in my childhood and sent many people with this purpose. Some of them were very delusive and others very powerful and canny. Only Pootana was humane and the very thought of killing an infant stopped her heart beat."

"Krishna, you your-self had killed all these messengers of death and never felt anything at that time, then why are you feeling restless now?"

"True, they could not harm me, but Kansa by using his propaganda-machinery was successful in my character-assassination to a large extent."

"I suppose that one of such allegations is that you exploited the moments of fun and frolics with Gopis and they gave it the name Raslila."

"Yes, that is."

"But you had left for Mathura with Akroor when you were less than eleven years of age, so the lie behind this is self-evident. Krishna, I remember, we together with others used to play many games. You used to play the flute so well that it always made us spell-bound. Very often all of us used to sing and dance collectively and at such moments my feet used to beat in rhythm as if they were out of my control."

"And Radhey do you remember that at the time of our return from forests after tending cows, our mothers used to assemble out of their homes and when we reached back they caressed our faces pouring their affection on us. Very often the people of Gokul and Vrindavan assembling in moonlight used to make celebrations with great fun and fare."

"Yes I do but Kansa publicised these as your Raslila; that is fun and humour with intent of exploitation. It was repeatedly spread so intensely that the learned and thoughtful section of society also accepted it."

"Radhey, in addition to this it was also publicised that Krishna when he was still a child, stealthily collected all the clothes of Gopis, who were taking bath in Yamuna and climbed on a tree. The naked Gopis when came out of the river, requested him a lot to get their clothes back.

The so called learned and thoughtful people of the society believed this false and malicious propaganda also, while our scriptures completely forbid naked bath in rivers and ponds and this is considered very much against the morals.

They accepted that these girls or women of our

society were very uncivilised and shameless. They assembled on the bank of the river, took-off all their clothes, entered into the river, took bath and came out, in the same position. Meanwhile a boy collected and climbed a tree with that huge lot of clothes, but none of them noticed it.

Whether all of them were very indifferent about their clothes or had closed their eyes or they had taken-off their clothes at a distant place, not visible from their position and walked to the river.

When they came out of the river, searched their clothes, located them with a boy on the tree, made several requests with the boy for their clothes and all this in a completely nude state.

No one of these women got anger, all of them were so much charmed towards a small boy that they tolerated all this insolence gladly and in the mean time no one else passed through that area. Was it the bank of a river beside a populated area or a totally desolated place?

In his attempt to defame me, Kansa did not bother the damage he was doing to the society and I am pretty sure that some people accepted and circulated this story only to cover their misdeeds."

"True," Radha said "This was an insult to the entire women-folk. No body could think as to why the cropping up of such stories stopped after the death of Kansa, is also surprising. The so called learned people of the society did not put a question mark on such stories, no dissidence was voiced."

"Radhike, these evil designs of my character-assassination did stop for some time after the death of

Kansa, but they again gained momentum with emergence of my new enemies. I freed thousands of woeful women from the custody of Bhaumasur. Some people call him Narkasur also.

These ladies were of different age-groups. I sent them to their homes but unfortunately most of the families did not accept them for different reasons. Then ultimately I gave them shelter and arranged for their dignified living but my enemies spread the rumour that I have married all of them.

A marriage with all of these sixteen thousand one hundred women would have been a very big event and could never be hidden from the eyes of the society.

This is only the propaganda-machinery of the people involved in my character-assassination which is telling that I have sixteen thousand one hundred and eight wives."

Krishna silenced after saying this and the calm spread. Radha looked at his face, held his hand and started walking. A little later she laughed gently and said,

"Oh, you yourself say that only a person treating pleasure and sorrow, respect and disrespect evenly, is a yogi. Then why this Yogiraj Krishna is sad on such petty matters?"

"Radhike, I am not sad, but yes I am worried about the wisdom of the people. If they consider me a human being, they should divide the number sixteen thousand one hundred eight by three sixty five; the number of days in a year.

A person going to a new wife per day will need more than forty four years to meet her again. He will forget her face even, in such a long period and will definitely confront her annoyance. The problem will be bigger with a person busy doing Rasleelas since his childhood with very little virility left and if they consider me an incarnation of God, do they think that only this type of works are left for God?

What type of God is in their imaginations and whether their God remains involved in this type of acts?"

Radha was a surprised listener of these logics and the calculation behind. She kept silently watching on his face. Krishna was opening his heart and voicing his pains.

"And Radhey, some people claiming themselves to be my devotee and a knowledgeable person put forward some blind arguments and call it an act of a god, that is me. They always further this discussion with support of some imaginative arguments."

Radha who was listening with admiration, said,

"Krishna you have created history with your great deeds, have shown unparallel virility, set highest standards in Yoga, knowledge and love without passion. Your impressions are there in every bright aspect of life. Are you worried about your infamy in future due to these stories?"

"Radhey, do you think that I will worry about my fame, infamy, respect or disrespect or any other obstacle coming in my way in performance of my duties?"

"No I don't think so. You are not called Yogeshwer (the master yogi) just casually or by chance. The cause of your worry must be somewhat different and very important one."

"Radhey, you have just said that I have created

history. My father was also saying something alike in the morning. Think, if this is true, if I have done so, the people may use these stories to become immoral.

These stories will give them a chance to ridicule our faiths. It will not affect me but may cause irreparable damage to our society.

I am also afraid that in the coming days, the people forgetting my preaching will entangle themselves in such cooked stories and start living an aimless life. If it so happens, it will become an obstruction in the development of the society, whereas I my-self have performed my duties forgetting about the pleasures and the woes, grace and disgrace throughout my life.

The basic concept behind whatever I explained to Arjun was that a person should never be averse to his duties.

The indolence is just like a poison for the society and these indolent people forwarding various reasons in support of their indolence spoil the society."

"I agree with you, but setting aside all these things I am in a different mood today and want to say something else. May I?"

"Yes, you are welcome."

"I see, you play flute, dance, give love, pilfer butter from the pot of Gopis, avoid unnecessary conflicts, fight against injustice and wrongs, preach and practise truth and integrity, know every thing, very knowledgeable and above all, are a great yogi.

You are never defeated but always a winner or a person behind the victory, never seeking the way but always showing the way.

You have never exhibited miseries; remain very indifferent and still very affectionate. You have numerous shades of personality and never a captive of any one shade just like other great or god-men in the society. You never stopped anywhere, gave pleasure of a loving child to your parents, the spiritual pleasure to me and a husband`s love to Rukmini. You had been a true friend of friends.

Actually you have been on the top of every aspect of life. I can not count your innumerable and shining shades, only salute them all.

I am sure that a person like you had never been and will never be on this earth. You are one and the only and there will never be a second Krishna in the history."

Krishna felt shy. He said,

"Radhey I know you are fun-loving and so are joking."

"Yes, I am fun-loving and to laugh is my nature, but here I am not joking. This is the voice of my inner-self. You are really matchless."

Just then an attendant came and informed,

"Lord, Nand Baba & others are waiting for you. All the preparations of the evening prayer are done."

Krishna, as if a person arose from sleep, said,

"Okay, I am coming."

And to his dismay he found Radha was nowhere, he was standing alone.

5.

When the Talks Begin

Krishna came down from the roof of the palace, found his parents and Rukmini waiting. Every one was ready for the evening prayers.

"I am sorry for this delay on my part. Now, please wait a little more, I am coming after washing my hands and feet to attend the prayer."

Krishna returned within no time and took a seat beside his mother and just then Deoki put a question before him,

"Krishna, I feel you remain very contemplative these days. If there is anything to worry about, will you not share it with us?"

"No Maan, there is nothing like that. No reason for any anxiety," he said, but Deoki did not look satisfied. She looked towards Vasudeo and Rukmini and found silent endorsement of her question in their eyes. They too had noticed the different from usual behaviour of Krishna but none had any answer.

The prayers started with chanting of mantras. When the mantras were over, Rukmini proposed,

"Let us start devotional singing. It removes tensions and pleases mind. Krishna will play the flute and we will do the singing.

Krishna took the flute, put it on his lips and a musical sound with almost intoxicating effects filled the atmosphere. Others started chanting, "Om Namah Shivay" in a melodious tone.

The heavy voice of Vasudeo mixed with two soft voices and the musical sound of flute gave such an effect as if the goddess of seven notes of music had come down her-self.

The echo of this voice and the fragrance of sanctity created an atmosphere full of divine pleasure and the goddess Parvati had to say to Shiv,

"Let us reach that place and we will remain their till the sounds of Kirtan; the devotional songs last.

Holding the hands of pleasure

The goddess of musical notes

Came down on the earth

The pious moments emitted fragrance

The echo invited Uma and Shiv

Prayers started from hearts

And it appeared as if

These moments are manifesting

The soul with divinity

And taking it to new heights.

Apart from the light of lamps, there was a different tingle also giving the entire place of worship a divine tint. A fragrance different from that of flowers and the sandal was there, it was mild and a little intoxicating with a touch of sanctity. Krishna knew it was due to Radha always present in his heart.

Some one came

Filled the body and the soul

With the fragrance of flowers

And the cool of slow blowing winds

When Kirtan was over Krishna put his flute behind him on the sheet of cloth spread on the floor. Rukmini lifted it, saving all the eyes and left the room saying,

"I am going to arrange water for you people."

She went out, put the flute with her lips and blew it softly. It sounded a little. She felt delighted but lest anybody should hear the sound, she stopped playing it and put it in her clothes, came back with an attendant with water, served it, took a seat near Krishna, took the flute out of her clothes and put it at its place beside him.

He noticed it, grasped her mind and smiled. After taking a few gulps of water he addressed his father,

"Tatshree, are both of you happy and contended? Actually your satisfaction in our prime concern.'

"Krishna, it is much more than that. Rukmini and you always give us a feel of fortune and pleasure Vasudeo said and after a pause he added -"But yes one thing is there which sometimes pinches us."

"And what is that?"

"Our daughter Subhadra is married to Arjun who is a cousin of Duryodhan. The entire dynasty of their Kuru-vansha was annihilated except Pandavas in Mahabharata. This great dynasty of Kuru-vansha had the glorious Bhisma and a virtuous Gandhari.

The great warrior, gallant, learned and best yogi of all the times our son Krishna was also there. He and only he was the hero of this war, but why did he choose, playing the role of charioteer of Arjun, did not stop this war and chose the very insignificant role of a charioteer for himself. These are the questions which often haunt our minds."

"Pitashree, these queries are very genuine and I know such questions will be there in the minds of so many other people also."

"Krishna, you will be enjoying a very prominent place and very tall stature in the history and the time will always be raising such questions before you."

"Okay, let me answer these questions."

"Yes, please speak out."

"Pitashree, you have raised the question of my relationship with Arjun, but the fact is that relationships keep breaking and recomposing according to the time and circumstances and your son remains with truth and humanity without consideration of any relationship.

Krishna is not charioteer of his friend and relative Arjun alone, but of every such person who is on the path of truth. So I suppose that the role of charioteer is very significant one.

Pitashree, if I had any such considerations in my mind I would not have done the job of collecting the defiled leaf-plate of people during the Yagyna performed by Yudhishthir."

"Yes, correct," said Vasudeo.

"And Pitashree you have said that I was the hero of that great war Mahabharata, but the fact is otherwise and I humbly urge that the only hero in this war was truth and it was the victory of the same."

"Yes I agree, it was victory of the truth, but it was possible only because of your patronage to it and therefore my son, you were the real hero."

-"But my patronage to Truth is always there. Pandavas won only because they were carrying the flag of truth and Kaurvas lost because they were carrying the flag of falsehood and that is why that even the great warriors like Karna, Guru Dronacharya, Bhisma Pitamah coupled with splendour and blessings of Gandhari could not save them from the disaster they met" said Krishna.

Deoki interrupted,

"The discussion between you, the father and the son is becoming grave. The ease of mind acquired after the devotional songs may disappear. This type of discussions should take place only after the meals. I am bothered about Rukmini, it has made her tense. Actually this is the time of dinner and so let us go for that."

Krishna smiled and said,

"Why is it so? Your daughter-in-law becomes tense on such petty matters. If she lacks understanding, please help her."

"I may or may not lack understanding but I understand you very well," Rukmini playfully said pulling lightly his clothe as a mark of protest and added in a low tone,

"Don`t consider me as naive as Radha. I will so hide your flute that you will not be able to trace it."

Krishna smiled and said,

"You have a lot of understanding, okay."

Vasudeo was ahead of all and indifferent, but Deoki listened and smiled on this conversation.

* * *

There were winds with fragrance of blooming flowers, the dew around on the leaves, soothing early morning light, chirping of birds in the widely spread garden of the palace and a beautiful temple with Shivling and idol of Durga on one side of it and a cow-shed on the other.

Some attendants were tendering and milking cows. Just then Rukmini arrived there, caressed cows, took a pot from one attendant, sat near a black cow and started milking it. Its young one looked at Rukmini. She fondled it and said,

"Oh, don`t bother, I will leave sufficient milk for you."

Deoki and Vasudeo were in the temple. Deoki had

collected some flowers from the garden. They together offered them to Shiv and Durga, closed their eyes and started chanting mantras. The atmosphere was full of sanctity. With eyes closed they were feeling its divine effects. When prayers ended, they opened their eyes, bowed in His memory, came out and started walking in the garden.

As the dawn knocked

Sun-rays arrived

Buds bloomed

The drops of dew shined

The prayers were voiced

And the gods awoke.

The bare-footed Deoki walking on the grass, her feet wet with dew and feeling the cool, looked at Vasudeo and said,

"Yesterday, our Krishna had become very serious. Why do you put such questions before him? He might have felt very uneasy."

"Deoki, I know that, but he has developed a giant-sized stature and not only the present society but also the coming tomorrow will raise such doubts. So let him answer these questions. I want his life to be like an open book."

"If you think so, it is okay. Look how many species of birds are here."

"Yes, but none is beautiful like a peacock. Apart from

being beautiful it kills the poisonous snakes also."

Deoki understood that he is having Krishna in his mind who wears feathers of peacock on his forehead, she nodded and said,

"Now I have got your motive behind putting such uncomfortable questions before Krishna. You want that just like legs of peacock there should be nothing indecent in his life," she said.

"Yes, you have rightly understood me," Vasudeo said.

"But are you satisfied with his answers?"

"Yes, but the main question is still unanswered and that is, why he did not stop that war. He was capable of doing so. That day the discussion was left incomplete," said Vasudeo.

"I believe Krishna will be having an appropriate answer to that."

"I too,"

After a pause, Deoki said,

"Do you listen to Cuckoo? It is so sweet that I always want to listen to it," said Deoki.

"I think that the Cuckoos of this garden sing sweeter than others," Vasudeo said.

"Why so," Deoki asked.

"May be, because they copy you," Vasudeo playfully said.

"Good jest," Deoki laughed.

Walking a little, they reached the cow-shed. When Rukmini saw them, she stood up, came forward, put the end of her sari properly on her head, touched their feet and they blessed her.

"Oh, you are milking the cow, but where are the attendants?"

"They are there, but I have taken this job on my own because I feel from the eyes and behaviour of this black one that it loves me. I have named it Kajari."

Deoki and Vasudeo laughed. Vasudeo asked,

"Is there any thing more?"

"Yes, the young-one of this cow, is of a few days only, therefore I my-self come to milk it and leave sufficient milk for this calf."

"Oh, this is really some thing good," Vasudeo said. Deoki looked at Vasudeo and elatedly said,

"She is my daughter-in-law," and then added,

"Shall we move towards sea-shore. I like the mornings there."

"Okay," said Vasudeo and they left. Rukmini too left after milking the cow. She had to monitor the arrangements of breakfast.

6.

Memories Pierce

It was a dull morning. Nand and Yashoda were in the courtyard of their house. Yashoda was preparing breakfast but mechanically. When it was ready she put it before Nand and said,

"Please have it."

"And you?"

"I will do take but you please begin."

"No, we will begin together," Nand said but after a while he added,

"Yashoda, did you notice one thing? Our cows are the same, trees are the same, eatables are the same and the hands cooking them are same, but there is no taste in anything as it was when Krishna was here."

Yashoda was moved at these words. She turned her eyes and bowed her head, a few drops of tears fell on the ground and Nand noticed it. It pained him a lot. He raised the head of Yashoda with his hand and looked into her eyes. There were tired and spiritless eyes on the either side. Nand took a cloth, wiped her tears and said in a heavy and choked voice,

"Yashoda, you are weeping but it is of no use. Try to adjust with the time."

"No, I am not weeping."

"But I see tears in your eyes."

"Nothing, simply his memories have struck and then this morning also seems to be very dull. Its melodies are lost somewhere."

"You are right, now the mornings are languid, the days are spiritless, the evenings are sad and nights don`t ask anything, they just come and spread out."

"He had been in my lap for about eleven years and was unable to sleep without clinging to me. Our days always started with his laughs."

"Yashoda, He is no more a child; our Krishna has grown up now. He is a big hero in the society, having various glorious achievements to his credit. He has built a new city Dwarika and is a king there."

"I agree and this is no less a pleasure to have a child like him and fortunately we had it but he still comes to my mind as a small child only.

Very often I am mistaken that that naughty boy is hiding somewhere in the house. It is almost impossible for me to forget him. He was the sprit of this house. The sun still rises but it does not light our house, it remains dark as usual." said Yashoda.

"I too feel alike, but we will have to have patience. The birds foster their young-ones with a lot of care and affection but once they are expert in flying, make separate nest for them and never return back to their parents. The world is like this only," Vasudeo said.

"But we are neither birds nor animals. We are human beings. Here parents and children expect love from one an other throughout their life. How can we be like birds and animals?"

"Yashoda, I believe that though he is away from us due to the circumstances yet the love for us will be still alive in his heart."

"The same belief is keeping me alive," Yashoda said.

"And to me too," came one more voice. Both of them were startled. They were so lost in their talks that they could not notice the arrival of a third person.

Surprised, they looked towards that voice. It was Radha. Yashoda picked up her hand and said,

"When did you come?"

"Just now," she replied, tried to smile and hide her tears from them. Yashoda drew her near, caressed on her back and asked,

"How are your parents, Kirtida and Vrishbhanu?"

"They are fine,"

-"Radhey, we are going to have our breakfast, please join us."

"Maan, I have already had. While passing through this way,I found your door open and came in."

"It is a favour to us. We find Krishna`s reflection in your eyes and it gives us pleasure and strength."

"But Maan, I find his reflection everywhere in this Gokul and Vrindavan and in your feet, too. Both of you have done great favour to me by not going to Dwarika."

"Radha, we can not leave this place. His memories are embedded here, so it is not a favour to you or anybody else. It was simply our helplessness and it is you who give us strength to sustain this sorrow.

We find our Krishna in your eyes and this is not our imagination or any illusion."

Radha lowered her eyelids. Tears welled up her eyes and stretching lines on her cheeks fell on the ground.

"Krishna is in the eyes of every person in Gokul and Vrindavan. Not only this, he is visible in every particle on the earth and even in the skies, of these places," Radha said, wiping the tears on her face with her fingers.

"This is no wonder Radhey. You find him everywhere because he lives in your eyes," Yashoda said.

"Yashoda, just now you were saying that we are not birds or animal," Nand said.

"Yes, I was saying so."

"What I feel is that we need to learn something from birds and animals. They do not nourish any futile affection or expectations with their young ones."

"Is it correct to call love or affection futile or non-futile?"

"Yes, it is. It is necessary till the children are young because in its absence, we will not be able to give due care to them but once they are grownup and self-dependant this becomes more or less irrelevant.

There are always some expectations from those

whom we love and their ignorance to us causes pains," Vasudeo said.

Radha was listening very peacefully and attentively,

"Baba, I want to ask one thing if you don`t consider it my impertinence."

"Yes you can. This is always your prerogative."

"Does any one calculate profit and loss in affection which develops on its own?

"Radhike, these calculations are always there, hidden in some corner of our heart and sooner or later become cause of our sorrows."

"But our affection with Krishna had no selfish motives. Had we any expectations from him?"

"Our expectations have so many faces. The desire that our loved one will not depart us is also the same."

"Kindly don`t make this morning more painful by these serious discussions. Our breakfast is lying just untouched," Yashoda interrupted.

"Oh, sorry Yashoda, let us have it and Radhe, you too will join us. Please don`t bother about the delay. I will accompany you home and see your father Vrishbhanu on this pretence."

"Okay Baba and Maan but please forgive me if I have added to your pain," Radha said.

"Oh no Radhey, this is not your fault but this is our destiny. You are always dearer to us than life," Vasudeo said.

One is tired of walking

But the woods of memories are long spread

The hidden expectations are piercing like thorns

The end is not visible

And the mind has become captive of these woods.

* * *

In Dwarika, the entire family; Deoki, Vasudeo, Rukmini and Krishna was sitting together after breakfast. Vasudeo stood up and said,

"Okay, I am leaving. I have got some verses on Shiv to read."

"I too am coming with you," said Deoki. Rukmini also got up and left. Krishna was left alone. Suddenly he felt some tears in his eyes.

Radha`s memories struck him. He comprehended, Radha has definitely wept somewhere and the tears in his eyes are hers only.

The great yogi closed his eyes and went in trance. The entire scene of Gokul comprising Nand, Yashoda and Radha came before his eyes and perturbed him.

Radha was no different from him as per her own statement, but the inability to share the sorrows of his fostering parents Nand and Yashoda pierced Krishna.

He remembered that Uddhava when went to Gokul, had tried to console Radha and her maids, but no one took care of Yashoda and Nand. Today, they badly need some support and there is none except Radha to show some affinity. Krishna felt he will never be able to repay her debt.

Suddenly Rukmini came and found Krishna sitting quiet and alone.

"Where are you?" she asked. It startled Krishna.

"It is nothing, only some memories of Maan Yashoda and Baba Nand are in my mind."

"Why don`t you bring them here?"

"You have put a natural question which may be striking others also and a very common perception may be that I am differentiating between my fostering and natural parents. Rukmini actually I had tried hard to bring them here."

"Then why did they not come?"

"They said, they can not desert the house where their Krishna has grown up. This is not possible in their life. Every corner of the house reminds them of my childhood. They say that it is a sacred place for them."

After a pause he further added,

"Their sentiments are so deeply attached with that place that I could not dare to shift them from there and simply gave up the idea."

"And Radha," Rukmini asked.

"Rukmini, do you envy her?"

"I can only say that you have not understood your wife. I have never envied her. You had left Mathura when you were less than eleven years of age. She has got nothing but for your memories since then. I find my-self nowhere before her devotion and sacrifice. I respect and only respect her."

She further added after a while,

"Murlidhar, you did not reply my question."

"What is that?"

"I had asked, why did you leave Radha, there."

"What rights had I on her? And look at the destiny, today Maan Yashoda, Baba Nand and Radha are the strength of one another. The regent of death alone can dare to separate them."

"Is the regent of death greater than you?"

"Today, you are putting such questions before me which are difficult to answer."

"Pardon," Rukmini said, wiped her eyes with fingers and gave a short smile.

"Rukmini, you are smiling and weeping simultaneously. How is it?" Krishna said and held her hands. Rukmini felt the warmth of those hands, breathed deeply and said,

"You will not understand it. Actually I am proud of my fate because I have been able to get you and sorry because even after passing so much life with you, I have not been able get you. So I am smiling but naturally there are tears in my eyes."

"What do you mean? You have me and yet you don`t have me. This statement has contradictions."

"No, there are no contradictions. It is very plain and simple."

It silenced Krishna. Rukmini took his hands and touched them with her eyelids then bowed down, touched his feet and left. Astonished Krishna kept watching her and she got away. Krishna in a contemplative mood went out of the palace.

A few dew drops
Resting on a flower
Tilted and fell
Pain hidden in the smiles
Spilled and touched heart.

7.

The Pages of Conspiracies

Krishna was worried. He was yet to reply the questions put before him. There was not much time left in his departure. Walking through the corridors of palace, he unknowingly reached at the doors of Vasudeo`s room, knocked lightly with his forefinger and called out,

"Pitashree,"

"Please come in," the reply came. Krishna entered. Deoki was also there. He touched their feet took a seat alongside them. Deoki said,

"Krishna, it is good that you have come. We were talking about you only."

"Maan, is there any thing special?

"No, a purpose is not always needed to remember you. We just love to talk about you."

"My good luck," Krishna said.

Vasudeo looked at his face and asked,

"Where are you coming from?"

"Pitashree, fortunately the state matters did not prolonged much and I was free, so I decided to come to you."

"Very nice of you Krishna, but it appears to me from your face that you want to say something."

"Correct Pitashree, yes it is so. Only the other day you had put some questions before me."

"Yes I did and the main question is still unanswered."

"Yes, that is, and if you can afford time, we can discuss it today."

"That's O. K."

"Let me also say some thing," Deoki addressed to Krishna.

"Krishna, you have started remaining very serious these days and you can not imagine how hard it hurts me? Is there any thing to worry about?"

Krishna tried to laugh loudly,

"No Maan, there is nothing to worry about. Every thing is just as usual."

"Krishna, Don`t show me prudence and I am not amused by this false loud laugh. I know you well. I am your mother."

"Yes and I am your child." Krishna got up and drew Deoki`s head close to his chest to show affection. After a while Deoki raised her head and started caressing Krishna`s forehead and hair.

"There is no one like my son," she said.

Vasudeo laughed and joined her, saying, -"Yes and none can ever be."

Then addressing Krishna he said,

"Krishna, now come to your reply."

"That day you had asked that why did I not stop the big war of Mahabharata and tried to avoid the huge destruction it did."

"Yes I had."

"Pitashree, I had tried. As per the terms and conditions of the gamble that took place between them, the Pandvas had completed their exile of thirteen years in forests and their state of Indraprasth was to be restored back to them by the Kaurvas but they refused.

I went to the court of Duryodhan on this pretext, on behalf of Pandvas and requested them for the same but Duryodhan turned down this request and ridiculed. Though his elders had tried to make him understand but he did not heed to their advice, started conspiring against me and tried to make me captive though he could not.

His father Dhirtrashtra, grand father Pitamah Bhisma and teacher Guru Dronacharya could compel him to accept the justified demand of Pandvas but for different reasons and motives they did not."

Deoki who was listening to this conversation very attentively, felt restless and said,

"Krishna I wonder how Duryodhan could think of taking you in custody. I feel he was not only wicked but a stupid too and Dhritrashtra, Bhisma and Dronacharya were not cowards so I will call their inaction as a silent endorsement of the whole affair."

"Maan, and this was so, when all of them knew that Kaurvas had won in that gamble only because of rascality of Shakuni, the maternal uncle of Duryodhan and Pandvas had tolerated this abuse of skill only because they did not want to create a scene in presence of their elders and moreover they accepted their exile in forest, only due to their commitment to honesty, otherwise nobody could dare to force them.

Dhritrashtra himself had become a party to the conspiracies of his son and brother-in-law Shakuni. Actually it was he who had called Yudhishthir to Hastinapur exploiting his position of being an elder of the family. It was with a hidden motive to defeat Pandavas in gamble and deprive them of their state.

Yudhishthir did come honouring the wish of Dhritrashtra, but he was against the gambling. He condemned it and said it to be the root of all the evils. He wanted to escape this offer but Kaurvas calling it to be his cowardice, ridiculed, challenged and provoked Pandavas, while Dhritrashtra observed a perverse silence in the matter.

Yudhishthir lost Indraprasth state in gambling and lastly very perturbed, challenged, offended and provoked was made to put Draupdi on bet. It was a plan to demoralise and insult Pandavas. Thus bowing to moral pressure, Yudhishthir unwittingly performed an act grossly condemnable and earning a bad name for him in the history. No one in that court opposed due to the fear of Duryodhan.

The gamble ended with a loss of state, twelve years of exile in forests and further one year of living in a non-traceable way for Pandavas. It was loaded with one more condition that if anyhow Duryodhan traced Pandvas in this last year they would have to pass another thirteen years in exile, with the same terms and conditions. Thus it was a plan designed to trap and annihilate Pandvas for ever."

"I think it was natural act of Duryodhan," Deoki said.

"He had inherited such perversity from his father Dhritrashtra and the maternal uncle Shakuni," she added.

"Maan, you are correct. Actually the state of Hastinapur belonged to Pandu, the father of Pandvas and they were the real heirs of that state. Vichitraveerya, the step brother of Bhisma had two sons Dhritrashtra and Pandu. Dhritrashtra was his elder son but was blind and not found suitable to become a king and therefore Pandu was given the throne.

He proved to be a glorious king but once, when he erroneously shot an arrow on a sage named Kindum, the sage died and this affected him deeply. He relinquished the throne, renounced the world and went to Gandhmadan hills to live. His wives Kunti and Madri accompanied him. Dhritrashtra became caretaker of the state. He should have handed over the state to Yudhishthir, the eldest son of Pandu at the time of his gaining majority but he did not, though he had a precedent in his own family.

Dhritrashtra's grandfather Maharaja Shantun had died when his son Vichitraveerya was still a child. Then Bhisma had managed the state, but only till he was a minor and had handed it over to Vichitraveerya once he gained majority.

Whereas Dhritrashtra exploited the opportunity in his favour, became the king and in due course of time declared his son Duryodhan as the heir of the throne.

He played the game very perversely and circulated the news that his wife Gandhari has given birth to one hundreds sons. It was a trick to gain in number game. Since it was impossible for a woman to give birth to one hundred children at a time, an unimaginable lie was told that originally Gandhari had delivered a round mass which was divided into one hundred pieces and each piece was put in a separate earthen pot. Then after two years, with the blessings of Maharshi Vyas each piece turned into a child and thus the one hundred Kaurvas took birth.

In a way it was a humiliation of Gandhari as well, but Dhritrashtra overlooked that point. If they were really one hundred, why there is no mention of their any act anywhere but for their death in the war of Mahabharata?"

Krishna finished, and Vasudeo who was a silent listener till then asked,

"His name was being dragged in such hypothetical episode but Maharshi Vyas did not protest. Is it not strange?'

"May be, because normally sages do not entangle themselves in any clash with the state authority, but there can be other reasons also and in this prospective we should consider one more event.

After the death of king Pandu it was Maharshi's idea that now Satyawati; the grand mother of Dhritrashtra, mother Amba and step mother Ambalika should leave the state and go to live in forests. This had ended the possibility of any truth coming to lime-light regarding his role in the birth of Dhritrashtra, Pandu and Vidur. Any discussion in this regard could bring it to surface.

Dhritrashtra had strongly supported this idea due to his vested interests.

Pitashree, one more action of Maharshi Vyas needs to be analysed. Draupdi was wedded to Arjun by her father Drupad. Maharshi Vyas went to that place uninvited and to her utter dismay pronounced a dictum that she should accept all the five Pandavas as her husband.

In this regard he had a story to tell. He told that Draupadi in her previous birth had worshiped Lord Shiv with great devotion for a husband having all the virtues but since it was not possible to get a single person as per her desire, Lord Shiv blessed her with five husbands in spite of her strong resentments.

Why Maharshi reached there to tell such a story about a newly wedded bride is yet to be understood, but it spread a thought of five husbands and that became instrumental in Draupadi`s character-assassination in later days and helped Duryodhan`s nefarious designs.

Maharshi telling the story unwittingly cut short the stature of Lord Shiv also. Probably great characters also commit big mistakes."

"But Krishna, Maharshi has criticised Kaurvas at several occasions," Vasudeo said.

"Pitashree, yes he has criticised them on several occasions but always in their absence. To criticize in absence is one thing and to register a protest is another. Moreover sometimes elders of family do criticise and scold their youngers, but whenever there is a matter of interest, they find the ways to support them and very especially when these youngers are in power," Krishna said.

"The inactive posture adopted by Bhisma Pitamah is also very confounding. He remained totally silent on the misdeeds of Kaurvas and never raised a voice against their gross injustices. He did not object to, even the ugly incident like an attempt to strip Draupadi. Did his conscious never pinch him?" said Vasudeo.

"Pitashree, what can be said about that? Here I remember that once Pitamah Bhisma and Guru Dronacharya had pursued Dhritrashtra to give the state of Indraprasth to Pandvas as a consolation. Dhritrashtra gave it unwillingly and he himself and his son Duryodhan wanted to take it back, some way or the other. That deceitful betting was organized to fulfil this purpose against their wishes, which became a cause of miseries for Pandavas.

So the silence of Pitamah and Dronacharya might have been due to their limitations shown by Dhritrashtra & Duryodhan at various occasions but still they were supposed to object with all their might against that ugly crime against humanity. Here, their astonishing silence was perturbing and condemnable.

"Krishna, there must have been some impact of these dirty tactics on the common man of Hastinapur."

"Yes it had," said Krishna, "The people from the very beginning of this Kaurav Pandav episode, were in favour of Pandavas and it had increased the feeling of insecurity in Dhritrashtra and that of enmity against Pandavas in Duryodhan. That is why they connived and sent Pandavas and their mother Kunti to the forests of Varnavart on the pretext of enjoying holidays.

There they were given a house made of highly inflammable material and that house was put on fire while they were inside. Somehow they escaped unhurt but had to stay incognito in forests for a very long time and apart from this, at two different occasions Duryodhan tried to poison Bhim.

To disgrace Arjun and to make him fight with Karna, Duryodhan declared Karna as ruler of a small state Angdesh. Dhritrashtra was a party in every act of Duryodhan to disgrace Pandvas and their mother Kunti and Bhism Pitamah can not be supposed to be always unaware of these acts.

Dhritrashtra was not only blind, but he had lost his conscience also. Gandhari had wrapped her eyes because her husband was blind but by not protesting against the misdeeds of his son Duryodhan, she had stopped listening to her soul as well."

"What do you want to say Krishna?" Vasudeo asked.

-"I have said it Pitashree. Not to protest against an injustice is both cowardice and guilt. Pandavas were protesting the injustice. Do you feel that your son would have played a silent spectator? Had it not been my cowardice and guilt?" Krishna said.

"Krishna you were right. Injustice must always be strongly protested, but you did not fight this war. You had gone there with a decision of not raising any arm. What type of protest was that?"

"I was present at every moment of that war as a charioteer of Arjun. To become a charioteer of some one means to carry him to the goal. I gave Arjun a vision to select the right goal, to abandon the cowardice-detachment and saved Pandavas from embracing a defeat without any fight. I was a very important and integral part of that war and since it was a sacrificial fire pit so the offerings were bound to be there," Krishna said.

"Yes, but those offerings were precious human lives. People blame you of instigating Arjun for this war."

"Naturally the offerings will be according to the need that be and I never instigated Arjun but only counselled him and ultimately left the decision entirely on him (Geeta, Shlok 63 Chapter 18) Pitashree, if to impart the knowledge of one's duties is a guilt, then yes I am guilty, otherwise I can say that the persons blaming have not understood me," he said.

"I agree and accept your logic, but putting a lady on stake in a gamble is no less a crime. Whether Yudhishthir and the other Pandvas can be absolved of that crime?"

"Certainly not. It was their crime and a serious one and had I been present there, it could have never happen. When Draupadi remembered me with a crying soul, I got the message without messenger, immediately rushed to that place and saved her from being molested.

Though Dushashan had taken hold of extreme upper part of her sari but he could not dare to proceed further in his nefariousness. My presence stopped him and when Pandavas were leaving, Duryodhan could not dare to take Draupadi in his custody or say anything against her dignity although he had won her in the gamble."

"Okay, but after such an act whether your support to Pandvas was proper? Vasudeo queried.

Deoki was silently listening to this conversation. She also joined and said,

"Krishna, it was not an insult of Draupdi alone but a disgrace to entire women community."

"Yes both of you are correct and history will never forgive Pandvas for this blunder but at the time of Mahabharata war when I stood with them, they had already paid dearly and undergone sufficient punishment for their misconduct. They had lost their state and pride, passed twelve years in wilderness in deep forests with Draupadi and spent one year as servants, incognito.

So on the one hand there was a party which had undergone severe punishment, repentant and sorry realising its fault and on the other hand there were organised conspiracies and the doers were proud of their acts," Krishna said.

"Krishna, you are correct but now it is too late at night. Let us go to sleep," Vasudeo said.

"Okay, it is really late. Mother and you need rest, but I have to make a request."

"Yes, what is that?" Vasudeo said.

"Pitashree it appears to me that this discussion is still incomplete and with your permission I will like to further it in the next sitting."

"Okay, we will shortly further this discussion."

Krishna touched the feet of his parents, took their blessings and left for his bedroom.

8.

Between the Lines of a Song

The river Yamuna was flowing peacefully. Some birds were chirping in the nearby cluster of the trees. There were dry leaves, some grass, and a few flowers on the ground. A few flocks of birds, in the clear and blue sky were returning to their nests. The bank of Yamuna, a place of merriment which normally remained very busy, was looking very desolate. The evening was descending. Krishna was standing there taking support of the trunk of a tree which was slanting and only a little above the ground.

He was full of thoughts with eyes on the horizon. So many faces and related memories were striking his mind. Just then he saw a human shadow approaching the river. When it came nearer it became clear that it was a woman. A little later Krishna recognized it was Lalita, a very close friend of Radha. He was surprised to see her all alone. He arose and walked towards her. When he reached nearer called,

"Lalite,"

Lalita looked at him and was startled,

"Oh, Krishna, is it you?"

-"Yes it is me, but how is it that you are alone? Why are others like Vishakha, Chitra and Sudevi etc. not with you and this place which always remained busy is looking so desolate?"

"Now-a-days, it remains like this only. Your absence is very much pronounced here, but when did you come? Have you met Baba Nand and Maan Yashoda? Does Radha know that you are here?" Lalita asked.

"Lalita, I have just arrived and was under the impression that all of you will be here, so straight forward I came to this place, but I could not dare to go home or meet Radha.

I have heard that Baba, Maan and Radha all are sad and displeased with me. I had come with the idea of startling them with my sudden arrival, but by the time I reached here, it appeared to me that it may create some difficult situation."

"You are correct. They may not bear with the pleasure of your sudden arrival."

"Lalita, how are they? I suppose Baba and Maan will be at home but I can not guess any thing about Radha. How is she? Is she very sad and hurt?"

"You, please come and see it your-self," Lalita said.

"Really, where is she?"

"Krishna, come with me," she said and started moving along the river side. After walking awhile

Krishna asked,

"Lalita, how far is it?"

"Don`t be so impatient. It is only a little far from here."

And after a little walk, the shadow of a human being appeared on the sand alongside the river. Krishna really became impatient. He wanted to rush and reach that place as early as possible. When they reached near Radha, found that she was lost in her own world looking silently at the stream of water. Lalita called her, saying,

"Radha, where are you?"

"Here only," came the reply.

"Look, who has come."

Radha raised her eyes.

"Radhey, how are you?" Krishna said.

Radha looked at the voice and surprise flooded her eyes. Her body moved in rapture, lips opened but she could not speak.

"Radhey, it is me," he said again.

"Really, is it really you, Krishna."

"Yes it is me, your Krishna."

The embankment of sentiments swept away, Radha wept.

O, my share of God

You have come, but too late

Innumerable drops of water

Starting from the mountains

And travelling a long way

Have reached and mingled with the sea

My eyes have searched

From earth to sky

A deserted heart

Lonely and alone

Sitting in the sand

With empty oyster-shells

Waits and worships

O, my share of God.

Krishna astonished and eyes fixed on her face, said,

"How is that, are you weeping?"

Sobbing Radha tried to control, picked his hand, bowed her head, touched it with her forehead and wept again. Krishna raising her head with his hands, said,

"Radhey, I can't bear with it. It is penetrating."

Lalita who was listening silently looked at Krishna and said,

"Now, it is getting late so I am leaving. Please take care of her."

She filled her pitcher with water and left, but moving awhile, she turned back and said humorously,

"Krishna, do you remember, you used to break our pitchers full of water?"

"Yes, I do," he laughed.

"Will you do it again?"

"Am I still a child?"

"No, but that child was God's favour to us." Saying this, she turned back and finally left. Krishna looked at her till she was visible, then picked up Radha`s hand who was still sobbing and said,

"Please come."

Together they reached near the stream of water and sat. Radha put her head on his shoulder. The evening was passing out and it was getting darker. One moon was there in the sky, the other one in the river swaying with its waves, but there was yet one more flawless moon sobbing on the shoulder of Krishna. He raised Radha`s head with his hand on her forehead. Radha looked at him and then dropped down her eyelids, tears starting from two beautiful eyes fell and rested on Krishna`s clothes. His patience was almost over and his eyes too were wet.

"Radhey, will you only weep and not talk to me?" he said. Radha could hardly stop her hiccups, nodded and said in a very low voice,

"Yes, I will," but putting a part of sari on her face she wept again. Krishna was moved and said,

"Radhey,"

"Yes,"

"How are you?"

"It is before you it-self."

"Very much displeased?"

"No, It is not so."

"Then why don`t you talk?"

"I don`t know what to say."

Then all of a sudden she smiled, wiped her tears and said,

"Did you not bring your flute?"

"Yes I have, I was coming to you and I knew that you will ask for it but Radhey, we have met after such a long interval. You have said about yourself with your tears, but instead of asking anything about me you are asking about the flute."

Radha gave a cute smile again and it appeared as if it was beauty in person present at the bank of Yamuna. The blushing moon hid its face in the clouds.

"That is my flute," she said.

"Radhey, nothing is divided between us."

"Are you feeling jealous with the flute?"

"May be. Radha when I was here and your maids used to say that Radha envies the flute, I could never believe it. I could not think of a person envying a lifeless thing, but today, I can understand it."

Radha put her palm on his lips,

"Don`t call it lifeless. While on your lips it does not sound but sings the best possible melodies. I have never heard such a tranquillizing music," she said.

"But I have," said Krishna.

"Oh really, but where" Radha was surprised.

"It is from your anklets."

Radha laughed and said,

"Who can win you Ranchhore (a Hindi word for one who leaves a battleground without fighting)?" Radha said humorously.

"Radhey, you will also call me Ranchhore without understanding the reason behind leaving that battle."

"How could I? Have you ever come and tried to make me understand the reason?"

"Actually there were many compulsions, but Radhey even your skewed talks are giving me a good feeling, at least they have made you laugh. Otherwise your tears had made me nervous."

"Krishna, I was not weeping out of any sorrow, but the tears in my eyes were due to the unimaginable pleasure out of your sudden arrival. And yes, please tell me the reason behind your escape from that battle. People call you Ranchhore and it hurts me immensely."

"Okay, let me tell you. The number of my enemies was not reduced even after the death of Kansa. Kalyavan from the south of Mathura and Jarasandh the king of Magadh were continuously attacking me. Kalyavan was killed at the hands of very glorious king Muchkund son of Mandhata from the dynasty of Shree Ram but Jarasandh whom I had defeated seventeen times in battles was not peaceful and his desire to ruin the entire Yadav clan was still furious.

The Dwarika was complete and the transfer of Yadvas to Dwarika was in progress so there was no point in putting on stake the precious human lives by engaging in more battles with him. Therefore the next time when Jarasandh attacked me, I fled to avoid the conflict," Krishna said.

Radha was listening carefully and when Krishna stopped awhile she looked at him with skewed eyes, smiled and asked,

"Oh, I have got your point, but whether it was the only reason or there was something more behind it?"

Krishna felt a bit shy on her slanting posture and the skewed question, laughed slightly and said,

"Yes, there was another reason also. Rukmini wanted to marry me but her brother Rukmee was adamant on marrying her with Shishupal. My engagement in battles would have made Rukmee successful in his nefarious designs and Rukmini`s life miserable."

After a pause he asked,

"Radhey, could I convince you?"

"Yes, of course, but only a little,"

"Only a little?"

"Yes and I will still call you Ranchhore."

"But Radhey, was I wrong in avoiding that confrontation with Jarasandh?"

"No, that was a wise decision and those who call you Ranchhore due to that reason have failed to understand you, but I am not taking the context of that battle."

"Then which battle are you talking about?"

"It is life which is also a battlefield. Krishna, once you left Gokul for Mathura, you did not come back. After penalising Kansa for his misdeeds, giving the royal throne of Mathura to his father Ugrasen and getting release of your parents Deoki and Vasudeo from the prison, you could have come here to meet us, but you did not.

What were you afraid of? You could never forget the love and affection you received from here and Krishna, to shield your-self behind your duties was also not possible.

So you, instead of coming, sent Uddhava after a long gap, who preached us to forget you. Was it not your escapism?"

Krishna was silent and non-pulsed. After a pause Radha added,

"And you could not stay in Mathura even. You left that place also and made your home in Dwarika near sea-shore and miles away from here. Had you lost the courage to live here and fight circumstances? Whether it was simply a search of peace or a desire to get away from some people?"

"What do you feel Radhey? Speak out and I will listen."

"Krishna, a small boy who made Kaliya run, raised Goverdhan hillock on his little finger and performed various acts of matchless bravery, who had power to change the circumstances in his favour, could never be afraid of any one."

After this Radha again stopped awhile and fixed her eyes on his face. Astonished Krishna was looking at her face, he said,

"Why do have you stopped Radhey?"

"Am I hurting you?"

"No, I know this is vent of your afflictions, so please continue."

"Krishna, when you had left with Akroor, we all had hoped that on some day you will be back, but you did not, and naturally with the passage of time our grievances increased. Though these were only out of love and affection, yet gradually they were beyond anybody's competence to redress. So Krishna you did not come back. What to call it if not escapism?"

Krishna saw her face red with impulse and eyes on the stream of river. He called,

"Radhey,"

"Krishna, how much water would have flown in this Yamuna since then?"

"I will not be able to guess."

"Okay, can you imagine how many tears would have flown in its stream?"

"No, but definitely they will be much more than my imagination," he said and then to change the topic added,

"Radhey, shall I play the flute? I have brought it here due to you only."

-"Yes, to listen to your flute is the height of fortune."

Krishna took the flute out of his clothes and was going to start playing it, suddenly Radha naughtily snatched it.

"Today, I will play it," she said.

Krishna laughed.

"Okay, my pleasure, but it would be imperfect without the sound of your anklets."

"I will not let it be so, but I will not return the flute."

"Okay. It is upto you'.

Radha sat straightening her legs towards the stream, and her feet touching the water. The river started washing her red lotus feet. She put the flute on her lips, blew it and her fingers started to move on its holes. She also started shaking her feet gently and the sound of anklets mixed with that of the flute. A very melodious sound echoed and filled the atmosphere. The beauty, music and the pleasure were sky high.

> *The waves of music*
> *With the ripples of water*
> *Danced and flew high*
> *So as to touch the sky*
> *The shine of beauty*
> *And smiles of flowers of Jasmine*
> *Filled the air.*

* * *

The very soft rays of the sun had arrived to tell that it is dawn. Rukmini looked at the face of Krishna and found him in sound sleep. Daily, Krishna used to arise early in the morning so Rukmini was a bit surprised. She gently called, then stretched her hand to touch and awaken him but stopped short and was spell-bound looking at his fascinating face. Just then Krishna opened his eyes,

"Oh, it is late, I was dreaming," he said.

"I had got it," Rukmini said.

Krishna arose, looked at the place where he used to keep his flute. It was not there.

Rukmini rose up and went out of the room. Krishna also rose up but remained in the bed. The dream of the night was still in his eyes.

9.

Radha; an Ever-Soothing Light

Radha. Who was she? Whether she was only the daughter of Kirtida and Vrishbhanu who lived in Barsana and a playmate of Krishna whom he could never meet after leaving Gokul at the age of eleven?

Whether she was just a human being, who was arrested in the platonic love of a person called Krishna and living her entire life with his memories only or something more than this?

Krishna deep in emotions felt, her devotion and relinquishment were always a great inspiration and strength behind his successes. It was she who maintained his peace and balance of mind even in the difficult times and most adverse circumstances. She was his wisdom and conscience and always with him.

There was love-inspired devotion between them. Had she been only a lovelorn beloved, she could have reached Mathura to meet him or at least she could have arranged to send a message. There was only a little distance between Gokul and Mathura.

They were a union of souls, physically apart but always together. Their separation was not possible.

The poets, devotees, persons with saintly nature and those with crookedness of thoughts have different images of Radha according to their own assumptions but the fact is that Radha is a character beyond all the imaginations.

Where ego is annihilated, love without passion crosses all the boundaries, the worshipper, the worship and the worshiped become one, the bondages and the salvation, the meeting and the separation become meaningless, Radha is there. She is always like a soothing light.

Rukmini was his fortune and auspiciousness, symbol of prosperity and magnificence. There was a tie of marriage between them but the relationship with Radha was above all the worldly ties.

Radha had to come though not physically to deliver peace whenever he was restless. She was a sheer bliss.

Krishna felt, probably this is why she was knocking his mind very frequently these days. She was eager and active to maintain peace in his mind.

Krishna rose up. The morning had come.

10.

Deep in Emotions

Krishna thought that the very intent of his arrival is fulfilled and the time of departure has come. He had started assigning his monarchial duties to others and that process was also almost complete. The administration and the economy of Dwarika were organised and well managed. All the administrative officers were competent in disposal of their work justifiably and were devoted to honesty.

Rukmini was very well looking after the internal affairs of the palace and well assisted by many inmates. She had learned a lot and was capable of skillfully handling the affairs of the palace. She was especially devoted to Deoki and Vasudeo.

Krishna had too much faith in her capabilities. He knew that she can well manage the administration also, of Dwarika in his absence but after his departure she could immolate her-self out of anguish. So he decided to request her to help in the management of his monarchial duties right from now and taking it as his wish, she may give up the idea of self-immolation. Still if it so happens, he decided to accept it as destiny.

His fostering parents had already adjusted themselves with the circumstances and his own union with Radha could never break off, no matter how apart they are. They were eachothers reflections.

Every action in one's mind knocked the other's heart. It was purely spiritual and not a physical relationship but he was bothered about Rukmini. How would she manage her-self after his departure was his worry? Krishna decided to make her mentally stronger and with this decision he experienced some relief.

Suddenly with a break of thoughts, he saw that it was just another evening as usual and he was unmindfully walking alongside the sea-shore. He noticed that he had come far off from the palace.

One attendant was following him. Krishna asked him to go back. The Nageshwar Mahadeo temple of Shiv was at a little distance. He started walking a little briskly so that he may return back in time. Rukmini would be perturbed if he is late.

After a while, he found himself at the doors of the temple. He touched the steps with reverence and entered the temple with folded hands in deferential salutation; sat bending his feet, folded his hands, closed his eyes, started meditation and went in trance. After some time he opened his eyes on the sound of some foot-steps. It was the priest. Krishna saluted him and the priest raised his hands showering blessings.

"God bless you Dwarikadheesh," he said.

"How are you? Is there any need or problem?"

"No Dwarikadheesh, no problem is possible in your reign," he replied.

Krishna once again bowed in deferential salutation before Shiv, came out of the temple and moved towards the palace but after a while his charioteer met him in the way with chariot. Krishna noticed and boarded it but was surprised.

"How could you know that I am here?" he asked.

"Sir, it was my guess. Firstly I went to the sea-shore but you were not there, then I concluded that definitely you will be in this temple to offer evening prayers," he said.

"Have you come on your own?"

"No sir, actually Rani Maan (he meant Rukmini) was very much perturbed since the darkness was spreading and you were still out. She asked me to go with the chariot, and search you out," said the charioteer.

The chariot was running on its way. The resound of tramps of horse was in the air. Krishna was thinking of Rukmini. She had used to remain more concerned about him, these days. He was continuously feeling that Rukmini has guessed some thing and was busy reading his mind.

The chariot stopped at the palace. Two attendants came running and stood with folded hands. Krishna stepped down and smiled at them. One of them was elder to him.

"Are you okay?" Krishna asked.

"Yes my lord, it is your kindness."

Krishna called the other one by his name,

"And you?" he inquired.

"I am also fine. Thank you, sir," prompt came the reply.

Krishna moved towards the palace. The gardener and his wife were approaching with flowers and a garland in a basket. They came near and extended it towards him. He accepted it.

"How are both of you?" he asked.

"We are fine sir. We are the gardener of Dwarikadheesh`s garden. No fortune can be greater than this."

Krishna moved with those flowers in his hand, but this statement of the gardener aroused a sharp headed question in his mind. Those who had fostered him, gardened his life will be happy or sad. His eyes became wet, but collecting him-self he entered the palace.

Rukmini was waiting. She hurriedly came, carried him inside. and gave him a seat. An attendant came out with a pot of water to wash his feet. Rukmini took that pot from him and asked him to go. She wanted to wash Krishna`s feet her-self but Krishna took hold of her hands and stopped her.

"Where were you? It is too late and I was very anxious," she said. Her pain spilled in her voice.

Krishna tried to laugh, extended his hand, gave flowers and tried to arrange the garland in her hair.

"It is beautifying you," he said.

Rukmini took it from his hands and properly arranged it in the braid of her hair. Krishna smilingly looked at her. Giving it a finishing touch, Rukmini said,

"You did not reply, Murlidhar?"

"I just went walking towards the temple."

"Which one?"

"It was the temple of Lord Shiv. Rukmini, when I was entering the palace on my return, I met the gardener and his wife."

"Definitely, they would have given these flowers to you."

"Yes Rukmini, you are correct and that meeting reminded me of Maan Yashoda and Baba Nand. They were my foster parents, gardening my childhood, but once departing from that place, I could not go there back to meet them and enquire about their well-being."

"What do you want to say? Definitely you are having something in your mind."

"Rukmini, I came off from Gokul and then from Mathura and never got time to look back. This had been my life."

"Are you sorry for that?"

"No Rukmini, I am not sorry for anything. I have always focused on my work, did what appeared me right and never bothered about the returns. The question of any joy or sorrow arises only when there is a desire of returns."

"But still you become sad on every mention of Gokul."

"Yes it is. The fact is that the people mould themselves according to the needs of the time. The residents of Gokul also did the same and with the passage of the time, they did not need my protection and then most of them have already come here and are well-settled, but Maan Yashoda and Baba Nand were so tied to the memories of my childhood that they refused to leave Gokul. Probably they have accepted my absence as their destiny, feel satisfaction in my achievements and may even be proud of me but memories of past still pain their heart."

"Now I have got your point. That pain hurts you also."

"Yes, you are correct and this is why, I can not forget them, but for the present leave it aside. Rukmini, I have to say something else to you."

"Yes please, I am eager to know that."

"Well Rukmini, today I was a bit late and you sent the chariot for me. Maan and Pitashree also praise you a lot. You don`t let them feel any inconvenience and I find that you are very well managing the other affairs too," Krishna said.

"You remain very busy with the works of the state so I have to look after these matters. This all is simply a part of my duty and there is nothing so special about it."

"I think, this daughter of Maharaja Bhishmak, princess of Vidarbh and the queen of Dwarika can share my monarchial responsibilities too."

Rukmini laughed and said,

"There is no need of such adjectives. I am always there to share your responsibilities, but as far as your monarchial responsibilities are concerned, you are there to look after those affairs, I don`t find my-self needed there and then these matters appear me above my reach."

"No Rukmini, nothing is above your reach and I really need your help. Many a times I feel that you could advice me better. You can contribute a lot in my works since you have the inherent qualities of a leader. It will be better if you can start it from tomorrow it-self."

"I can not disregard you in any way and to be with you in all the walks of the life is my duty. Moreover it will give me more time to be with you and it will be my pleasure, but tell me one thing. Are you planning to go some where? I find that you remain serious these days and always remain lost in some thoughts. I am worried."

"For the present, I am not going anywhere, but to go on one assignment or the other is part of my life."

"Lord, please tell me the truth. I will not be able to bear with your separation."

"Don't be impatient Rukmini, for the present I am not going anywhere, but I want you to help me from to-morrow it-self." Krishna took hold of Rukmini's hands and added,

"Rukmini, I badly need these hands."

"These are yours only," she said.

"I know," he said and touched his eyelids with her fingers.

"Please give a word," he added.

"Okay, please speak out."

"You will manage the affairs of Dwarika in my absence."

"I assure that I will always take the decision according to time, place and circumstances," she said.

Her reply silenced Krishna.

11.

The Women Considerations

It was afternoon and Krishna had returned to palace a bit early finishing his day's work. He was in a relaxed mood and restful posture in his room. Just then Deoki and Vasudeo came walking to that side. Krishna rose, touched their feet and seated them along his side. Luckily Rukmini too arrived, paid regards to her in-laws and finding all of them present there she said,

"Let me arrange some fruits for you."

Deoki interrupted, -"Rukmini you just sit with us and ask some attendant for this work."

"Okay," Rukmini said, went out and asked an attendant for the same, then came back and sat nearby.

Vasudeo started the dialogue,

"Krishna, you are early today!"

"Pitashree, the work was over so I decided to come

back home."

"You did well. Now you will be able to give us a company for some time, otherwise you remain very busy these days."

"Well Krishna," Vasudeo added,

"Our discussion on Kaurvas and Pandavas was left incomplete that day. Shall we start it now?"

"Yes, why not," Krishna said.

"You people become very serious in this discussion. It perturbs me," Deoki said.

"Deoki, the truth must come out. That day I felt that some people have kept it in dark, its voice is being suppressed and the lie is on a high pitch. Our Krishna is trying to reveal the truth. His act is laudable and beneficial to the society," Vasudeo explained and asked Krishna to continue.

"Pitashree, Kaurvas had not only occupied the Pandvas state by deception, they were busy in the character-assassination as well, of the women-folk. In the reign of Kaurvas it started from Satyavati; the grand mother of Kaurvas and Pandavas and it went up to Draupadi," Krishna said.

Deoki was surprised at this statement and said,

"Krishna, It has made me curious about the facts. Really to say that a woman has five husbands is nothing but her character-assassination only."

"Maan, you are correct and this is why I want a detailed discussion on it."

"Well, please begin," Deoki said.

"Maan, king Vichitraveerya was alive for many years

after his marriage, still if he had expired without any issue, then any issue of his wives Ambica and Ambalika with the union of some other male could never be his issue and consequently not a natural heir of the throne in that male-dominated society.

Adoption of a virtuous boy could also serve the purpose, but it is said that the queen mother Satyawati had requested Bhisma to give birth to a child with any of the wives of Vichitraveerya.

Since Bhisma was bound by his oath, he suggested the name of Mahrshi Vyas who was said to be the son of Rishi Parashar and Satyawati her-self when she was still unmarried. In a way it was a secret of her life and to disclose it was disgraceful act and an offence on her dignity.

Bhisma bothered about his commitment to throne, maintained his oath but forgot about the dignity of Satyawati; his step-mother. Prior to this, he had abducted Ambika and Ambalika for marrying them with his step brother Vichitraveerya.

The act of hurting the dignity of women-folk had started from here it-self. The heir of the throne could be a boy only, but who could predict that the coming baby will be male only. Still Maharshi Vyas agreed to this proposal. The reluctance of Ambika and Ambalika was not given any consideration. It was a gross injustice to them and very disgraceful too.

It was a very harsh decision and very much like their marriage, this time again their willingness or unwillingness was not assigned any value.

At the time of the very act, Ambika closed her eyes in

anguish and Ambalika turned pale due to fear and Maharshi predicted that the child of Ambika would be blind and that of Ambalika would be a patient of acute jaundice whereas a child can never be blind or an acute jaundice patient due to these reasons. The height of pain of these ladies on these deplorable prophecies can be well imagined.

Such an offensive and unpleasant prophecy was not needed also. This was not to serve any purpose. Whereas, it was ethical or unethical is debatable, but it definitely added insult to injury.

Maharshi had gone there to give birth to the heir of the throne. The son of a maid servant could never be an heir of the throne. He knew it well, still he gave birth to a child with the union of a maid servant also, on the pretext of fulfilling her desire. That lady did not show any non-cooperation and Maharshi prophesied that her child would be virtuous and a talented one.

It puts a big question mark on his behaviour. Whether this entire act was in conformity of his stature? Whether the ladies are not human-beings, but only an object whose willingness or unwillingness has no value?

He did not give any importance to the Draupadi`s protest against acceptance of five husbands, on the pretext of her prayers of her previous birth. And lastly, if there was any conspiracy to take the advantage of his stature, why did he not oppose it."

"Krishna, what you are saying is not new, but it is a different vision," Vasudeo said.

"Pitashree, more incidents of this type where dignity of women was not given any consideration continued till long," Krishna said and further added,

"The common man of Hastinapur was not happy with the coronation of Dhritrashtra. They wanted Yudhishthir to be their king due to his virtues. This situation was unpleasant and painful for Dhritrashtra.

Actually Dhritrashtra and Pandu not being the real sons of Vichitraveerya were not the natural heirs of the throne in that male dominated society. Pandu had established him-self as ruler by his valour, skills and character, whereas Dhritrashtra was not only blind but had nothing to do with propriety or impropriety.

After the death of Pandu, Maharshi advised to Satyawati, Ambika and Ambalika to go to the forest and live there   only on the pretext of increasing sins, deception and guilt and decreasing moral values in the society.

Even if it was so, Dhritrashtra being the ruler of the state was responsible for the same. Moreover it was a matter of care and comfort of his mothers & grandmother, but he very shrewdly turned a blind eye to it.

The silence of Dhritrashtra can be understood because he was used to impropriety and deceptive behaviour. The departure of his mothers and grand-mother was going to help him in a way, in establishing him-self as an heir and a ruler of Hastinapur thereby, but Bhism also kept silence in this episode.

It perturbs and makes his behaviour difficult to understand.

Pitashree, this is a tale of compelling women, use them with selfish motives and then get rid of them."

Deoki was listening attentively to the entire

conversation, endorsing his arguments and was feeling proud of his son. She looked at Krishna and then at Vasudeo with eyes full of appreciation for Krishna.

Krishna noticed it and felt encouraged.

"Pitashree, these Kaurvas had tried character-assassination of Kunti and Madri also in a very planned and disgusting way."

"How is that, Krishna," Vasudeo asked.

"Pitashree, when renunciation of this world emerged in Pandu's mind, he had left for Shatshringa hills for austerity. His wives Kunti and Madri had also accompanied him. They lived there till the death of Pandu. Pandvas took birth there only.

Madri had immolated herself in the funeral pyre of Pandu but forbidden Kunti from doing so for the sake of fostering of their children who were still very young. Kunti who was all alone retuned back to Hastinapur with these children.

Dhritrashtra who was assigned the task of the caretaker of the state in Pandu's absence had already declared himself as the king of Hastinapur. Now lest the Pandvas should claim their right to the throne, Dhritrashtra circulated the rumour that Pandvas were not the sons of Pandu but of different deities.

This was not only an attempt to erase the right of Pandvas to the throne but also a dirty trick of assassinating the characters of Kunti and Madri to spoil their image in public eyes. Whereas to get celebrated, brave and virtuous sons aunt Kunti (she was sister of Vasudeo) had devoutly performed adoration of God for one complete year, king Pandu had done it standing on only one foot before the sun for the same period, and Madri had prayed Ashwini Kumars for the same, during that period but Dhritrashtra publicised that Kunti knew some mantra (a mystical verse) chanting which she could invoke any deity to get a child from him.

He propagated that Yudhishthir was the son of Yamraj; the deity of death. Those involved in this rumour mongering could not think that who will call Yamraj sitting on a terrifying he-buffalo, if he is in his senses, because Yamraj is known to award death whenever he comes.

As per these rumour mongers Kunti had invoked Vayu; the deity of air to get Bhīma, Indra; the king of deities to get Arjun and taught this mantra to Madri also who had invoked Ashwini Kumars with its help and got Nakul and Sahdeo.

If this mantra was so powerful and delivering what was the need of those difficult adorations of God by Pandu, Kunti and Madri. The deities blessed, can be understood, but to say that they physically appeared to give birth to a child, cuts their size and is in accusation of both the deity and the lady. It was a fantastic and unparallel imagination.

On the height of this villenss, during the war of Mahabharat, when Kaurvas were losing ground, it was propagated to boost up their moral that Karna was son of sun-God and Kunti of the time when she was still a virgin.

It was also added that Kunti on my behest had approached Karna in the darkness of night, begged for the life of Pandavas and told him that actually she was his mother, but could not own him for the fear of public slander.

It was yet another attempt of character-assassination of Kunti, downgrading her in the eyes of her own sons and demoralise the warriors on Pandva`s side. Very clearly, it appears to be a brain-child of some very crooked mind," Krishna said.

Rukmini who was listening to this conversation silently, could not stop her-self and asked,

"And Draupadi,"

"Yes, she too was a victim of such conspiracies. She was daughter of king Drupad and born with divine traits. That is why, people started saying that she was born of the oblation fire-pit.

Apart from Arjun, Duryodhan and Karna had also joined as her aspirants in her Swayamver (a custom in which the bride chooses her husband among her aspirants, assembled at one place). The qualifying condition of this Swayamver was very difficult and like other kings Duryodhan had also failed.

When Karna arose to try, Draupdi refused to marry him due to his non-elite background. Arjun was successful in hitting the target and the king Drupad married Draupdi with Arjun. Duryodhan and Karna felt hurt and insulted.

Since Dhirtrashtra also was anxious for the marriage of Draupadi with his son Duryodhan, this marriage filled all of the three, with revenge and with the malicious intentions so they aired the rumour that Draupadi had become wife of all the five Pandvas.

Aunt Kunti was especially targeted by the Kaurvas since she was the real king-mother and highly respected amongst the people. She asked Pandvas to share Draupdi as a material and Pandvas and Draupadi agreed to it, taking as their mother's words was yet another rumour spread with ill-intentions.

While all the Pandvas were virtuous and brave, there was no hindrance in their proper marriage, it was not a female-dominated society and there was no polygamy among women in practice, still to say that a lady like Kunti will ask for such an unnatural act, was totally baseless.

Actually Pandvas while living in forests used to bring some edibles every evening. That day they had come with Draupdi and told their mother that they had brought some thing very special. Kunti, without looking at it, presumed that it would be some material as usual and advised them to distribute it among them-selves.

Draupdi was not a material and this advice of Kunti was not for a human being. The distribution of a woman was not possible.

To take the words on the face value and leave their spirit behind has devastating effects.

Draupadi was Arjun's wife and Kunti had uttered those words erroneously so there was nothing wrong in making a correction. Will a mother unknowingly asking his sons to jump in a marsh, let them jump into it only to keep her words? Had Kunti and her sons no conscience?

Actually Duryodhan was trying to make rift between Pandavas and could get success in it by spreading this rumour and it was easy since all the Pandvas were living together under one roof. Otherwise Yudhishthir was wedded to Devika and Youdheya was his son, Bhim was wedded to Balandhra; the daughter of Kashiraj and Servag was his son, Nakul was wedded to Kareshumati and Nirmitra was his son and Sahdeo was wedded to Vijya and his son was Suhotra, still they shared Draupadi as their wife is a highly condemnable thought.

Then as if it was not enough, Kaurvas in a very planned manner made Pandvas put Draupadi on bet in gamble, won deceitfully and then insulted all of them in a crowded assembly," Krishna finished and became silent.

"Bigger the size, more are the efforts to cut it down. Who kicks a dead dog? Draupadi was one of the pre-eminent figures of her time and so the worst possible offences were made against her," Rukmini said.

There was mum awhile. It had left everyone contemplating. After a little later Krishna added,

"Pitashree, at the time of Rajsuya Yagyna of Pandavas, Draupadi had passed a comment on staggering Duryodhan that blinds give birth to blinds. This seems to be a much uncivilised remark in the first instance but Duryodhan had blemished her of being wife of all the five Pandvas.

This was a disgusting blame. To call him blind was a very natural and gentle reaction of that lady and was not untrue.

Leaving aside the physical blindness of Dhritrashtra, he was blind towards his duties as a ruler in infatuation of his son and Duryodhan was blind in his arrogance.

"Maan, Vidur was the son of a maid so Kaurvas never assigned any importance to him and though Dronacharya was his teacher, a great archer and a warrior but the truth is that he was a protégé of the state. But even Bhisma-

Pitamah never protested against this mentality and the injustice.

With committed loyalty to the throne of Hastinapur, he kept watching mutely, the insult of ladies of his own family. What should it be said? Whether history will forgive him of his total inaction despite his competence?" Krishna said.

"But there is a bright side also of these events which tells us that to follow the path of truth and justice is not a futile exercise," he added.

"Krishna, what is that?" Vasudeo asked.

"In this entire chain of events, people of Hastinapur and of the erstwhile area never believed these frivolous talks and even their love and affection for Kunti, Madri and Pandvas did not reduce. This is not a small thing."

"True and it proves that Pandavas were on the path of truth and justice," Vasudeo said.

"Krishna, I also want to say something," Deoki said.

"Well Maan you are welcome."

"Krishna, I feel Dhritrashtra and Duryodhan were the persons of very crooked mentality. They always considered woman as a thing and not as a human being.

Had it not been so, Dhritrashtra would not have allowed Gandhari to pass her entire life with eyes tied with a strip and live like a blind.

He could say that though he was blind yet he will not let her live like a blind and he will see this world through her eyes. He could pursue, appease or bound her with his love if he so wished. Being her husband it was his duty also, but sorry, he made no efforts in this regard.

Duryodhan was the eldest son of Gandhari and enjoyed her immense affection but he also did not make her understand the reason and give up her self acquired blindness. Moreover he never gave any importance to her advices. It shows that Gandhari was only a material and not person, for both of them.

This is yet another example of Kaurvas giving no value to the sentiments and the pains of women-folk," Deoki said.

Every one had finished and the atmosphere had become very serious. The eyes of Deoki and Rukmini were wet. Vasudeo put his hand on Krishna`s back, caressed and said,

"Krishna, I am convinced & endorse your views. Really it was a fight against immorality & astrocities. A holy war.

Pandavas get their state back was important but still more important was the end of mentality of considering woman as an object."

12.

Before The Departure

It was a time of complete solar eclipse. Since such occasions come rarely, Krishna and his elder brother Balram planned that people from Dwarika and those of Gokul and its nearby areas may assemble at a holy place Samantpanchak situated in Kurukshetra and celebrate performing rituals according to the occasion. Thus apart from celebrations it will also give them an opportunity to meet one another and some old memories will be revived. Pradyumn was the son of Krishna.

It was decided that Aniruddha; the son of Pradyumn and Kirtiverma; the commander of the army will stay in Dwarika for its safety. Many chariots were arranged to take the people to that place.

When Krishna reached Samantpanchak he found that Baba Nanda, Maan Yashoda, his childhood friends and acquaintances and Radha`s parents Kirtida and

Vrishbhanu were also there. Krishna met each and every person with affinity. Maan Yashoda embraced him and wept. Krishna could hardly stop her. Baba Nand was also very sentimental. Krishna touched his feet and Nand embraced him. Kirtida and Vrishbhanu were also with them. Krishna touched their feet as well.

It was a touching scene. Every body wanted to see and if possible, to touch him and Krishna was also in obliging mood.

Many closers and seats were arranged to perform Yagyna by offering herbs in the fire. Most of the people were on fast, still there were arrangements of snacks and meals. The Yagyna started and people began to collect around to perform rituals and offerings. Deoki, Vasudeo, Rukmini and the mother of Balram, Yashoda, Nand, Kirtida and Vrishbhanu were in the first row. After they finished, Rukmini, Krishna, Balram and his wife performed the rituals.

When they finished, Krishna arose and alongwith others started looking after the arrangements and meeting the people.

During this entire event Krishna`s eyes were busy searching some one. Rukmini noticed this restlessness of Krishna. She carried him towards the gathering of women from Vrindavan. Radha surrounded by her mates Lalita, Vishakha, Chitra, Champaklata, Sudevi, Tungvidya, Indulata, Rangdevi and others was busy in some discussion. Krishna asked Rukmini to take care of them and he him-self again started meeting the people.

When Rukmini reached there, they stood up as a mark of respect. Radha took hold of Rukmini's hand, embraced her and took her in her circle. Rukmini sat there and within no time mixed with them. A little later Radha and Rukmini looked very close to each other as if they were very old friends meeting after a long interval.

It was a festive atmosphere. Though Krishna was physically present there, yet mentally he was some where else, so he went a little away from the gathering and the memories of Radha besieged his mind and heart.

It was said that Radha was found under a tree, on a lotus in a pond. Vrishbhanu passing through that way saw her. Considering her to be a blessing of God, he took her in his hands and brought her home, put in the lap of his wife Kirtida and said,

"Lo, goddess her-self has come to our home."

Kirtida looked at her face loved her and said,

"In her appearance she really looks like a goddess. Where did you get her?"

Vrishbhanu narrated the story. Kirtida again embraced her and said,

"She is really a goddess, adornment, adoration and adorable every thing. We are blessed by God."

"You are true Kirtida. Definitely she is embodiment of some goddess. Shall we name her Radha," Vrishbhanu said.

"Radha! what does it mean?"

"I have taken 'Ra' from 'Raka'; that is moonlight and 'Dha' from 'Dhara'; that is stream. Join the two and it becomes 'Radha'; that is stream of moonlight. Actually, she looks like that.'

"Oh," Kirtida smiled. -"Really it suits her."

Krishna remembered, he had heard this story a number of times at Vrindavan. He looked at the side where Radha was sitting with her mates. She was not there. He went towards the side where Yagyna and rituals were being performed and he proved to be correct. Radha was there.

They caught each other's eyes. Krishna felt embarrassed and stood aside. Radha noticed it, stood up and moved out of the convention ground. Krishna followed as if he was tied to her. Rukmini noticed it, became apprehensive, bit her lips, smiled but said nothing.

Radha getting away from that place moved towards densely-situated trees at some distance. Reaching there she found a pond with some lotus flowers. She stopped and looked back. Krishna was behind her. Astonished Radha said,

"Oh, you."

"Yes, me." Krishna replied.

"Krishna, have you performed all the works?" she asked.

"Yes, they are done."

"Then,"

"Then what?"

"What is next?"

"It is time to leave."

Radha and Krishna were facing each other. Radha took his hand and said,

"Krishna, that day I had called you Ranchhore, escapist etc. You must have felt it,"

"What are you saying? How could you imagine that I can feel it?"

"Krishna, as a matter of fact, to avoid hindrances, I my-self had advised you not to return back to Gokul till the completion of all your works and I my-self was complaining to you a lot for not coming back. Actually, Vrindavan appeared so deserted and lifeless that it pained a lot and many a time I got moved."

"I can understand your anguish. I too had to bear a lot of pain.'

"I know," Radha said and added,

"Krishna, the flute was your permanent companion. It had filled Vrindavan with music. The absence of its music had created a big void in our hearts. Whatever is beautiful and musical, is it's creation. It makes life worth living. That day I had taken your flute too saying that I will not return it. The emotions had dominated me and I could not maintain my-self."

"That was not needed Radhey. These are the feelings which make difference between a human being and a machine and the tunes of this flute are your voice only. Why are you differentiating between you and me?"

"Yes Krishna, truly there can not be any such difference," Radha said and took his fingers in her fist.

"How beautifully these fingers play the flute! Krishna I am leaving. Can I take this flute with me? I will feel nice," she said again.

"It is yours," Krishna said, looked at her, peeped in her eyes and added,

"I too am coming very shortly."

"Krishna come. We will sit on the side of this pond for a while," Radha said, then added,- "I had heard the sound of your flute for the first time, it was default for me to believe that one can play it so well. Krishna I feel lost in the intoxicating sound of this flute."

"Radhey," Krishna said.

Radha smiled a little but with pain in her heart.

"Krishna, I want to listen to your flute once more, before leaving," she said.

"Okay," Krishna said and together they sat on the side of the pond. Radha gave the flute to Krishna. He put it on his lips and a very melodious but sad note reverberated and filled the atmosphere and the hearts. It reminded Krishna that only a little earlier he had said that its music was nothing but the voice of Radha.

Definitely it is voicing the Radha`s pain. Krishna kept playing it and Radha silently and attentively listening. After a while Radha interrupted,

"Krishna,"

He stopped playing the flute, found there was a little trembling in her voice. He looked at her face. The eyes were wet on both the sides.

"Krishna, take care of Rukmini, till you are here. She is wise, brilliant and of loving nature. You are fortunate to get her as your wife."

"Yes I know."

After a pause she added,

"Krishna, now you may leave, people at the convention ground must be looking for you."

"Radhey, you want to send me off."

"No, this is not true but for the sake of duties, we have always struggled with physical fascination. Now, is it good to yield to it at this last moment? We never met for bodies and our souls never separated. Now you go and let me leave," Radha said.

And she held the hand of Krishna holding the flute, lightly opened his fist holding the flute and took it in her hands.

"Radhey, it is true. This fascination is afflicting us in these last moments," Krishna said.

"So, shall I move?"

"Radhey," Krishna said. His throat was stuck and he could not say anything more.

"Krishna, will you do one thing for me?' Radha said.

"Yes, but what is to be done?."

"I had just said that I want to carry your flute with me.'

"Yes, you had."

"But that is not possible."

"Then."

"I want to leave this world listing to that intoxicating rhythemic sound of your flute."

"Krishna did not reply to it, only looked at her with his welled up eyes and trembling lips."

"Krishna, you look sad. Are you?" Krishna again did not reply.

"Krishna, please remember your own preechings. The soul is immortal and this life is a journey and here I want to end this journey with a happy note. Please help me."

"Radhey, to play the flute in those moments will be very difficult and painful as well."

"I know that but for my sake," Radha said but her voice was choked.

"Okay I will do it.' Krishna said. He took the flute, put if on his lips and started playing it.

"Okay, Krishna, I am leaving,"

Radha said and went behind the grove. A little later a ray of light emerged from there and went into the sky. Krishna understood that Radha has left. He stopped playing the flute, wiped his eyes and walked slowly in a contemplative mood.

Like a clear ray
Pleasant smell
Holy thought
Calm and silent
Someone came
And left as well.

Rukmini noticed the return of Krishna, the redness of his eyes and the absence of Radha. She got the gravity of the situation but observed mum as any questioning could pain Krishna more.

13.

Towards the Departure

A fowler, named Jara used to live his life by hunting birds and animals. It was his routine like so many other fowlers, but he was very much disturbed since last few days. He was unable to understand the reason, but one thing was clear. These days, his wife was requesting him to give up this profession of killing innocent birds and animals.

She wanted him to do some thing else for their livelihood. She was feeling very bad of this hunting business. Jara was unable to understand as to what has happened to her and why just all of a sudden she had started asking him to leave this family business. Her persuasion had developed a feeling in him also, that this is not a good business, but the problem was that he did not know any other work for his family's livelihood.

Today when he was coming out of his home with the

bow, arrow and the net, his wife interrupted,

"You are going again to take some innocent lives. It gives me feeling that my meal is mixed with their blood. Why don`t you start some other work?"

"You are correct and since you have started forbidding me, I am also feeling that this is not good job. To kill these innocent, hoping and jumping creatures is cruel, but what to do to earn our bread? I don`t know any other job.

"Once it has come to your mind, we will definitely be able to switch over to some other job. You can become a woodcutter and I will help in selling these woods in the market. I know mending of clothes and I can mend clothes of our neighbours and earn some money or else we can become labourers."

-"You are correct. We can find some other way to earn our livelihood."

"Then please leave arrows, bow and the net and let us start from today itself."

"Okay, I will leave this net here. So many birds are trapped in it and it becomes a pretext of taking many lives. I will go with bow and arrow, kill one animal only and manage with that."

"No, leave this bow and arrow too. We will go and seek some other work, be it that of a labourer."

"Yes we will, but not from today. Please give me one more day. May be, we don`t get a job of a labourer immediately."

"If it is so, then let us go to our king Dwarikadheesh. He will definitely help us. He can give us some work also."

"You are correct, if need be, we will go to him also, but today let me go for the last time. I have decided to hunt a deer today. Its meat and skin fetch handsome prices. Then we will be able to purchase a good axe and our routine will change from tomorrow. I will adopt the job of a woodcutter and you can start mending of clothes of our neighbours."

"But I feel that you please don`t go for hunting today it-self, lest you should shoot your arrow at some innocent creature. Let us go to the city and we will definitely get some job."

"No, let me go for today only and from tomorrow I will leave this job as per your wish. I don`t know why but today something is pushing me towards the forest as if I have to finish some incomplete work or there is some old score to settle. Please don`t stop me today. It appears as if someone is forcing me to go and I am unable to resist it."

"Okay, I can not force you, but it appears to me very inauspicious."

"I am a killer, nothing is auspicious or inauspicious for me and don`t bother I will return soon with a big deer."

"May God save us from any more sins," said the fowler`s wife and stood helplessly watching at him.

* * *

The morning knocked softly at the doors and Krishna arose and it seemed as if he was not sleeping, but only waiting for the dawn. He looked at the face of Rukmini sleeping aside, very calm and in deep sleep, the splendour of her face was competing with the shine of the morning. Krishna arose, but kept in mind that it should not disturb her sleep, came out of the room and went to become fresh. When he returned back Rukmini was awaken. She asked surprisingly,

"Today you have arisen so early. Do you have to go somewhere?"

Krishna felt confounded at this sudden question. Although he had decided to leave, but any affirmative reply could raise other difficult questions. He could not tell that he has decided to leave this body today and an answer in negative was to be a lie. He kept mum.

These days Krishna used to remain serious and this had already disturbed Rukmini, now this silence, made her more restive. She repeated her question,

"Do you have to leave early today for somewhere?"

Now Krishna had to reply but he got its answer imbedded in this question, he said,

"Yes, I have to go, but the purpose of my early rising is that I want to go for a morning walk with you in the garden and then together we will go to the temple. There we will be able to meet Maan and Pitashree and get their blessings too. We will go to the cow-shed also. Your pet cow Kazari has started recognising me also. I want to see her and her young one also. It all will be pleasurable.

"I too would feel nice. You please just wait a bit. I am getting ready in a few moments. For me, there can be nothing better than your company. It will be my fortune," Rukmini said and wanted to leave. Just then Krishna said,

"Okay, I will wait for you under the Ashoka trees just

outside the palace."

"Okay," Rukmini said and she left. Krishna came out and started walking under the Ashoka trees waiting for Rukmini. It was early in the morning and there was dew on the grass. Krishna's feet became wet and blows of winds were filling his clothes. He was feeling good.

There were flowers around and so the winds were fragrant and their touch with the body was refreshing. There were some flowers scattered on the ground. Krishna was trying to save them from coming under his feet.

He had moved a little far from the Ashoka trees but then he returned back so that Rukmini could easily locate him. He looked towards the sky. There were a few rays of light and the sun was trying to come out of the coverlet on its face.

When he was under the Ashoka trees it suddenly struck his mind that in her previous birth Rukmini as Sita had passed more than a year in distress, waiting for him under such trees, and just then Radha's memories struck him.

Her entire life had passed in waiting. Now she had already left this world and his time to leave, has also arrived. They will be able to meet only on the other side of this world.

Just then Rukmini arrived. She had put on a red sari and was holding a pot with stuff needed for rituals of adoration. She picked some flowers from the garden and put them also in the same pot.

Both of them moved together and stopped at the doors of the temple. It was between densely planted trees.

They raised their hands and rang the bells of the temple. Krishna was going to enter the temple just then Rukmini stopped him, took hold of the corner of the cloth Krishna had on his shoulders and handed over the adoration-pot to him. Krishna looked a little surprised.

He found that Rukmini was knotting it with the upper corner of her sari. Krishna, bluish like the sky, Rukmini bright like moonlight, a knot between the red and yellow clothes, the Shivling in front and a glorious idol of goddess Durga behind it, the sun which was rising slowly, came out speedily on the scene to watch that evident beauty.

Looking at Rukmini tying the knot, Krishna smiled and asked,

"Oh Rukmini, what are you doing?" he asked.

Rukmini with blushing face and smile on her lips said,

"My wish,"

Then Krishna did not say anything more. Rukmini after tying the knot took the adoration-pot from his hands. It appeared from her face as if she was convinced that now, Krishna can not go away from her.

They performed the worship with all the rituals and came out of the temple. A little girl, the daughter of the gardener, was there. Rukmini called her near and asked to open the knot. She did. Krishna patted her on her back and put some money in her hands.

Just then Deoki and Vasudeo arrived. Rukmini and Krishna expressed their regards touching their feet. While they entered the temple, Rukmini and Krishna waited for them outside. When they came out, all of them moved towards the cow-shelter. There Rukmini and Krishna stopped a short. Deoki noticed it and said,

-"Rukmini, if you people want to stay here you can, but we will move and yes, I am preparing the breakfast today so don`t get worried and you can take your own time."

"Okay Maan, but we are coming soon," Rukmini said.

She stayed there with Krishna. They reached near Kazari; the cow, fondled it and the calf. The cow raised its head and expressed fondness. An attendant came with a pot; Rukmini took it, sat on the ground, put the pot between her knees and started milking the cow. Krishna was fondling the calf and looking infatuated at the spell of Rukmini`s beauty. In the mean time Rukmini raised her head, caught his eyes, saw the feeling of love, blushed and said,

"What are you looking at?"

Krishna with a mischievous smile said,

"Your face,"

"But why, am I looking very beautiful?"

"You always look so."

It brought smile on her face. She said,

"Thank God, at least you are in a pleasant mood today."

In the mean time her attention diverted and milk spilled on the floor spoiling her sari also. Rukmini stopped milking, rose, came nearer and complained,

"See, the milk has spilled and spoiled my sari. It is due to you."

Krishna laughed at it, said,

"Oh sorry, but it was not due to me. It was due to your spell-binding beauty. Now let us move, Maan and Pitashre must be waiting for us."

Rukmini looked at him with skewed eyes, then skewed her lips too and said,

"Okay," but after a pause she added,

"Can we not stay here a little more? Your smiling face is fascinating me. I want to look at it for some more time."

Krishna felt shy. He said,

"I too am feeling very nice. Let us move towards the temple. There we will sit for a while on the grass in front of it."

Saying this, Krishna took hold of Rukmini`s hand, together they moved towards the temple and sat in front of it on the grass there.

"It is so nice here," Krishna said.

"Ya," Rukmini replied. Krishna looked towards the temple, the trees around and then at the sky. It was clear, blue and spread all over. He took a deep breath as if something very serious was running inside him. Just then, he felt a very silky touch and found that Rukmini, with eyes on his face, had put her hand on him. Krishna felt those eyes. He called,

"Rukmini,"

"Hum" she said and looked in his eyes. Those glowing eyes shook him somewhere deep inside. There was love, grievance and an attempt to read something. Krishna could not face those eyes, lowered his eyelids, took hold of Rukmini`s hands and said,

"Rukmini, you sing very well. Will you please sing for me?"

"Do you really want it?"

"Yes,

"ok," she said and started singing in her very melodious but low tone. Slowly she became louder, but only a little later she toned down her pitch.

It appeared as if she is not only singing, but also trying to say something. The song underlined her pain, it said,

"You are stubborn with a slanting foot in my heart, can never come out and your any attempt to go away will definitely turn me into a body without soul."

When the song was over, silence spread and a hollowness filled the atmosphere. Too much pain was spilled.

Krishna got the message but for the first time in his life, he felt helpless. Both of them were left speechless.

Suddenly there was a sharp voice of some bird, it startled them. They stood up and silently moved towards the palace.

When they reached, Deoki and Vasudeo were waiting for them. The breakfast was ready. There were fruit, butter and some dishes prepared by Deoki. Rukmini served it to others, but did not take it for her-self. Deoki noticed it and said,

"Rukmini, serve for your-self also and join us. There is no need of waiting."

Rukmini nodded and served for her-self. Krishna was full of praise of each and every item. It gave pleasure to Deoki. Even after the breakfast was over, no body was in mood of leaving. They started chatting.

The talks started from the childhood-pranks of Krishna at Gokul and Vrindavan, covered the killing of Kansa, Shishupal etc. and the important events of Mahabharata and lastly the making of Dwarika.

While discussing Dwarika, Krishna praised the efficient management of Rukmini. Krishna, him-self was a yogi and was above all the attachments but still he wanted the well-being of Dwarika and its inhabitants even after his departure, so he wanted Rukmini to take the administrative responsibilities of Dwarika. He had faith in her capabilities and as per his wish she had started taking interest in these matters.

Krishna was feeling contented. The services of Arjun were also available to guard the interests of Dwarika.

Still Krishna was contemplative. Memories were continuously haunting and so many scenes were flashing in his mind. Moreover he was very much perturbed imagining the plight of Rukmini after his departure.

After a while Deoki and Vasudeo left for their room. Rukmini and Krishna were left alone. Rukmini looked at Krishna's face and asked,

"Are you bothered for any thing?"

"No, I am not,"

"But some thing is definitely there."

"No, Rukmini there is nothing like that."

"Okay, if you don't want to tell, let me speak about your worry."

"Okay," Krishna laughed mildly.

"You are thinking that all the works to be done in this birth, are complete and so, you have decided to leave this body."

It completely astonished Krishna. He said,

"What are you saying Rukmini?"

"Why, am I wrong? And if it is so, it will be my greatest fortune. I don`t want to be correct."

"No, you are not wrong and then I can not speak a lie, but whether it was the reason behind tying a knot with me before performing the prayers in the morning."

"Yes, I could not do away with that fascination. At least it gave me one more chance to feel you having tied with me."

"But how could you know that?"

"It was simple. Your behaviour had changed a lot since last few days. You had started taking more care of me and giving me more importance. You were giving more time to your parents, sparing your-self from the monarchial duties and the day you wished me sharing your administrative work I was startled.

I tried to read between the lines and it became clear that you are about to leave."

"But Rukmini, still you behaved so normally. You did not let me feel that you have read my mind."

"Yes, because any change in my behaviour could have its impacts. It could make people guessing a lot, increase your tensions and worries, but could never change your decision."

It filled Krishna`s heart with emotions, he came forward, held Rukmini`s hands and said,

"Rukmini you have always taken care of my needs and accompanied me in every walk of life without bothering for your-self and once again you have proved your-self."

"Lord, you have decked up my life. Had you been a little late I would have been married to that crooked Shishupal."

"It was never possible since I was there," Krishna said and then added after a pause,

"Rukmini, really you are pretty good."

"Good or bad, but I am yours."

"Rukmini"

"Lord"

"The time of our separation has come. Probably only this much time was in our destiny, Please give me a send off."

"There is no point in sending you off. Only our bodies are separating but not our souls. Who can separate Luxmi from Narayan?" Rukmini said and tears streamlined on her cheeks.

"Rukmini, I have to go."

"Okay, you do, but I will not be able to stay here after your departure."

"What are you saying? Do you intend to become sati, immolating yourself after me?"

Rukmini put her head on his shoulder and wept bitterly. Krishna caressed and tried to raise her head. He wanted to look at her face but Rukmini did not raise it from his shoulder.

"After today, I will not get this shoulder to rest my head," she said.

"Collect yourself Rukmini. Really no one can separate us; not even the death of our bodies, but the very idea of immolation is unfair and immoral. Suicide is a sin, Rukmini."

"I don`t know virtue or sin. I know you only," said Rukmini and weeping bitterly embraced Krishna setting aside all the hesitations and shyness.

Krishna could not find any answer. Radha had already left and he was leaving. He knew that Rukmini will not be able to stay after it, but the idea of her self-immolation was very disturbing. He was moved and wanted to make her understand that it was highly immoral but he was pretty sure that Rukmini was not ready to take this advice.

Then he decided to leave the incidents taking place after his departure on the destiny it-self. He remained static for some time with Rukmini in his arms then firmly took a decision, softly separated her, held her face between his palms, looked in her eyes and said,

"Rukmini, for the whole life you had been my strength and weakness, too. Now, bid me good-bye."

"Lord," she said, bowed down, put her head on his feet and sobbed. Krishna raised her with his hands and when she stood up, looked at her face, tried to console her and then looking into the void he left. Rukmini followed him a little then stopped, became static and looked at him till possible.

Krishna, listening to the sound of breaths and sobs, turned his face, looked towards Rukmini and with the feelings of pain went ahead.

* * *

No food was prepared today in the house of fowler Jara. The evening had passed but her wife had not lit any lamp. Children had slept hungry. Both the husband and wife were sobbing sitting in the darkness.

Today the fowler Jara had shot his arrow on the red sole of the foot of Dwarikadheesh Krishna taking it to be head of a deer. The poisoned arrow had given him a pretext to leave his body and while leaving he had said to Jara,

"Don't be frightened or sorry. These are the ways of destiny………."

Someone left in a fashion

As if he had come

But only to leave

And the marks of his feet

Deep, shining and ever lasting

Were left, not only

On the canvas of time

But on this earth, the sky

And the hearts as well.

EPILOGUE

Krishna occupies a unique place in Indian history and tradition. Hindus have accepted him as an incarnation of God, but keeping in view the sprit of present scientific age, people want to know if he really existed. The European scholars put a big question mark on his existence and gave a preconceived view that he is a myth. Apart from this the British Sanskritists, due to their superior views about themselves, had developed the idea that the much of the Vedic beliefs, practices and legends have been incorporated from Bible and the stories of Jesus.

However the Heliodorus column was the archaeological discovery that proved to the disappointment of such people that the knowledge of Krishna, Mahabharata and the Vedic traditions predated Christianity by hundreds of years.

This Heliodorus column is situated at 45-minute ride from the Buddhist site Sanchi on the road to Vidisha. Locally it is known as Khamb Baba pillar. This was erected by Heliodorus, the Greek ambassador to India in 113 B.C.. Heliodorus was sent to the court of King Bhagbhadra by Antialkidas, the Greek king of Taxila. The kingdom of Taxila was part of the Bactrian region in the northwest India, which had been conquered by Alexender in 325 B.C. The area under Greek rule included Afghanistan, Pakistan and the Punjab of the present time.

Heliodorus has written on this stone pillar, the time it was erected and the fact that he had converted to Vaishnavism and started worshiping Lord Vishnu. The inscription on the column, as published in the Journal of the Royal Asiatic Society, says,

-"This Garud column of Vasudeo (Vishnu), the god of gods, was erected here by Heliodorus, a worshiper of Vishnu, and an inhabitant of Taxila who came as Greek ambassador from the Great King Kasiputra Bhagbhadra; the saviour, then reigning prosperously in the 14th year of his kingship. Three important precepts according to this inscription, when practiced lead to heaven, are the self-restraint, charity and the conscientiousness."

This shows that Heliodorus had become a worshiper of Vishnu and was well versed in the texts and the ways pertaining to this religion. How many other Greeks would have converted to Vaishnavism can only be guessed if such a notable ambassador did. This conclusively shows the Greek appreciation for India and its philosophy.

It was Alexender Cunningham who while doing an archaeological survey in 1877, gave significance to this column. However, he did not attend to the inscription on it because that was covered with vermilion and was not readable. Again it was in January 1901 when one Mr. Lake uncovered the paint from what he thought was some lettering. The ancient Brahmi text on it became visible. It was translated and the historical significance of the column became apparent.

The Heliodorus column also indicates that the Vedic traditions accepted converts at that time. Only after the difficulties between Hindus and Muslims, there was hesitancy on the part of Hindus to accept converts to the Vedic religion. We also have records from Greek travellers who came to India following Alexander's invasion and have left references about Krishna.

Authors like Pliny referred to Krishna as Heracles, based on Hari Krishna. They record that Heracles (Krishna) was held in special honour by the Sourseni tribe (Shoorsen was the grand father of Lord Krishna) and in such places as the major city of Methora (Mathura).

The Greek records go on to say that Heracles (Krishna) lived 138 generations before the time of Alexander and Sandrocottas, which was about 330 B.C. The calculations considering about 20 years per generation indicate roughly to 3090 B.C.; which is almost the right time considering 3102 B.C., the date when Kali-yug began.

The greatest barrier to a rational study of ancient Indian history continues to be a nineteenth century colonial fiction known as Aryan invasion of India. When the ruins of Mohenjo-Daro and Harappa were discovered, this was followed by new pieces of fiction known as Aryan-Dravin wars. Science has now fully discredited the both. The decipherment of Harrapan and pre-Harrapan scripts by some more scholars has taken Vedas to long before 3500 B.C.. Panini the great grammarian mentions several Mahabharata characters in his works.

Amongst Buddhist works Kunala Jataka mentions Krishnaa (Draupadi; the wife of Arjun), Bhimsen, Arjun, Nakul, Sahdeo and Yudhittila (Pali word for Yudhishthir). Dumkari Jataka makes mention of Dhananjay (Arjun) and Draupadi's Swayamver.

Krishna himself is mentioned in Surapitaka and Lalita

Vistara. Although these works are hostile to him, but show that he was accepted as a historical figure. They did not deny his existence.

A seal found in Harappa speaks of two essences; the Upanishad and the Sankhya philosophy. Gita is essentially the summary of Upanishads combined with rationalism of Sankhya Philosophy. God is indestructible, eternal and flow of life and that is Krishna.

It is really very strange that people of western Garhwal observe every year Duryodhan-festival and many believe that the city of Varnavart where Duryodhan tried to burn Pandavas alive, was situated in that locality.

It is also striking that at certain places people offer water in memory of Bhism during Shraddha; the Hindu ritual. The point to be highlighted here is that, had all these been poet's fancy and myths, as said by some section of scholars, the traditions could not have continued for such a long time.

Mr. M. Witernitz in his 'History of Indian Literature' writes, "History is one weak spot in Indian literature. It is in fact non-existent." The renowned German scholar Max Muller in his work 'History of Ancient Sanskrit Literature' writes, " No wonder that a nation like India cared so little for history."

What the writer of these lines feels is that history of India and that of Hindus dates thousands of years back and the present way of writing history and preserving it was not developed in those days. So whatever is available is mostly in the form of lyrics, but to deny the very existence of that civilisation on this basis only, is grossly unfair and depicts a biased mentality.

The philosophers and scholars of that time wanted to preserve the heritage, the history and the events in the life of Krishna for future generations and therefore they held a convention in the forest of Naimisharanya (a place near

Lucknow, India). Those seers had foreseen the present age of degradation and that the foreign invaders would destroy our culture. So they discussed all the stories and Vyas; one among them, wrote everything down.

This should also be kept in mind that scores of books preserving old heritage were put on fire at various places, by the foreign invaders. In India, Nalanda and Takchhshila universities of that time had met the same fate.

There are many proofs of the existence of Krishna in the various archaeological finds. A few of them are given below.

About 15 kilometres west of Mathura there is a well in a small and unimposing village Mora. In the year 1882 General Cunningham discovered a large stone slab filled with inscriptions, on the terrace of this ancient well. Although more than half of the writing had already peeled away, on the right side, the remainder was legible. It was transcribed and a facsimile of the inscription was published in the Archaeological Survey Of India`s annual report. A scholarly research of this inscription had made it evident that not only Krishna but his elder brother Balram (Sankarshana), son Pradyumn, grand son Aniruddha and Samba were being worshiped centuries before Christ. The Mora well inscription is an important archaeological proof of Krishna`s existence.

Furthermore, the Ghosundi inscription, found in the village Ghosundi in the Chittor, Rajasthan largely duplicates the message of the Mora well inscription. Kaviraj Shyamal Das brought this evidence to light in The Journal of the Bengal Asiatic Society. This inscription can be inspected in the Victoria Hall Museum in Udaipur.

This inscription in the form of Sanskrit script, called Northern Brahmi script, belongs to second century B.C. and is either of the late Maurya or early Sung periods.

An almost identical inscription was uncovered nearby

and is called the Hathi-vada inscription.

The same point is made, in the famous Nanaghat Cave inscription, in the state of Maharashtra where Krishna and Balram are included in an invocation of Brahma. This inscription shows further that the Vaishnava religion was no longer confined to the north India, but had spread to the south and had captured the hearts of the sturdy people of Maharashtra, from where it was destined to spread to the Tamil region and then reached with renewed vigour to the remotest corner of the Hindu Vedic World.

The excavations of Al-Khanum along the border of Afghanistan and the Soviet Union conducted by P. Bernard and a French archaeological expedition, unearthing six rectangular bronze coins issued by Indo-Greek ruler Agathocles with script written in both Greek and Brahmi, depicting image of Vishnu or Vasudeo carrying chakra and a pear-shaped vase gives another proof in his support.

Additional evidence that can help establish the time of Lord Krishna was at Mohenjo-Daro, where a tablet dated 2600 B.C. was found which depicts Lord Krishna in his childhood-days.

These examples show that he was popular at least prior to this date, but this not being my subject; I leave it here for the researchers.

On January 5 & 6, 2003, scholars from across the world came together, for the first time, in an attempt to establish the 'date of Kurukshetra war based on astronomical data' at the Mythic Society Bangalore and there was an amazing collection of information.

Dr. Raja Ramanna, M.P. and an eminent nuclear scientist delivered the inaugural speech. The well-known historian Dr. Surya Nath Kamath in his presidential address explained the objective as an 'exploration of authenticity of dates using planetary software and textual evidences containing over 150 references'. He emphasised on the need of 'Chronology for history.'

There were many other dignitaries present in this conclave.

The statement of Maharshi Vyas in Bhism Parva which states that "Amavasya occurred on the thirteenth day and the two eclipses in a month in Kurukshetra during the war" was also analysed using Lodestar-Pro-software.

Dr.B.N.Narahari Achar (Department of Physics, University of Memphis, U.S.A.) gave a brief description of available planetary software, a review of various works of astrophysicists Kocher, Siddharth and the astronomers Sengupta and Shrinivas Raghvan. Further he gave various astronomical references from the epic.

He critically examined the limitations and reliability of simulations and concluded that the astronomical events in the Mahabharata belong to the period of 3000 B.C. His conclusion was very very near to 3067 B.C., the period arrived at by Raghvan.

Various other learned speakers also spoke on the occasion relating to the ground truth of river Saraswati of Vedic times with the historicity of Mahabharata.

I hereby give dates of a few events of Mahabharata arrived at by Dr. Narahari Achar, Prof. Raghvan and some other researchers, correlated with planetary positions described in that epic, as far as possible.

Lord Krishna's date of birth comes around: Jul. - Aug. 3156- 3157.

(According to the daily The Indian Express, 26th Aug. 2013 was 5125th birthday of Lord Krishna and thus the year of his birth comes around 3112 B.C. which is near the year given above.)

His departure from Upalavya Nagar to Duryodhan on his peace-mission: Sep. 26, 3067 B.C

Krishna reaches Hastinapur: Sep. 28, 3067 B.C.

Lunar-eclipse: Sep. 29, 3067 B.C.

Karna accompanied Krishna to some distance in return journey on: Oct. 8, 3067 B.C.

On the way he described the Lord the position of planets in the sky and expressed the apprehension that such a planetary configuration stood for very bad omen: such as large scale loss of lives and drenching of blood. Maharshi Vyas narrated all these planetary positions in as many as 16 verses as if someone was describing it after visualising them in the sky.

Solar eclipse: Oct.14, 3067 B.C.

Krishna's elder brother Balram leaves on pilgrimage along the banks of Saraswati: Nov.1, 3067 B.C.

Mahabharata war starts (Dr. K. S. Raghvan and his co-worker Dr. G. S. Sampath Iyengar, using the planetary software came to the same conclusion): Nov. 22, 3067 B.C.

War continued till the wee hours of the morning: Dec. 8, 3067 B.C.

Balram returns from pilgrimage: Dec. 12, 3067 B.C. Winter solstice: Jan. 13, 3066 B.C.

Bhism's passing away: Jan. 17, 3066 B.C.

Krishna lived for 126 years and five months:

Departure of Lord Krishna and Kaliyug starts in full potency: Friday, Feb. 18, 3031 B.C. at 14 hours 27 minutes and 30 seconds.

(These dates are in conformity with the popular belief that Lord Krishna passed away 36 years after the war).

Kali-Yug starts in the mid-night: Feb. 17-18, 3102 B.C..

The famous astronomical text known as Surya

Siddhant states that the sun was 54 degrees away from the vernal equinox when Kali-yug began on a new moon day, which corresponds to the mid-night of Feb. 17/18, 3102 B.C at Ujjain (75 deg 47 min E 23 deg 15 min N).This is very near and supportive to the above calculations.

After shooting the arrow at his feet when the fowler 'Jara' approached Krishna, his last words were,

-"DON`T BE FRIGHTENED OR SORRY. THESE ARE THE WAYS OF DESTINY...."

Maharshi Vedavyas composed the main Vedic texts in around: 3000 B.C.

Maharshi Vedavyas composition contained only 8800 verses and was given the name 'Jai'. Later on Rishi Vaishampayan enlarged it to contain 24000 verses and he called it Bharat. Still later, many more verses were added to it and it was named Mahabharata.

The river Saraswati dried up or disappeared around 1900 B.C.

The period between the dates, Dec. 8, 3067 B.C. (the day of Bhishma`s fall) to Jan. 17, 3066 B.C. (the day of his passing away), is 48 days. However it is generally accepted that he lived 58 sleepless nights before his departure. If one counts those 10 days also that he led the Kaurav army into the war, in which he may have not been able to sleep, it would lead to the figure of 58 sleepless nights.

The year of departure of Krishna 3031 B.C. is in conformity with the signs given in the epic. Krishna had observed that omens similar to those seen at the time of Mahabharata war indicate the total destruction of Yadu clan. Astrological simulations show that 36 years after the war in 3067 there was an eclipse season with three eclipses closely falling on 20th Oct; the lunar eclipse, 5th Nov. the solar eclipse and 19the Nov. the partial solar eclipse in the year 3031 B.C., at the Anaparvani time and are consistent with the popular belief that he passed away 36 years after the war.

Dwarika, whose ancient name is Shrithirth also, was submerged in devastating cyclone only after 7 days of his departure and the entire Yadu-clan almost ruined.

In 1985, the under-water excavation discovered two submerged sea walls, a few meters apart and 20 to 30 ft below the sea-bed. 'The Hindu' dated 21st. Feb 1985 reported that Dwarika, the 'gateway' of ancient India, was submerged four to five thousand years ago.

It was significantly explained by Shri C.S. Mahadevan of Madras. According to him Dwarika was partially submerged in 3031 B.C. and Lord Krishna was born on July 26, 3112. It may be noted that Dwarika submerged in the sea, very shortly after Krishna's departure and therefore this is in total agreement with the date of his departure and very near to his date of birth given above.

Another person Arun Kumar Bansal worked out that Krishna was born on July, 21, 3228 B.C. and passed away at 2.00 P.M. on Feb. 18. 3102 B.C. (thus July; as the month of his birth and Feb.; as the month of his departure are confirmed in three different calculations) and according to him Kaliyug is supposed to have started and Dwaper ended on this date.

Aryabhatta, one of the great mathematician and astronomer of India in the 5th century, examined the astronomical positions recorded in the Mahabharata. In his work Aryabhatiya, he calculated the approximate date to be 3100 B.C. justifying the date of the Kurukshetra war to have been about 5000 years ago.

This again identifies and is very near to the year 3102 B. C.; the year arrived at by calculations in the text Surya Siddhant and those made by Greeks and Dr Narahari Achar and others.

A well-accepted fact, by both eastern and western scholars is that the present Kaliyug began on the midnight of 17-18 Feb. 3102 B.C. which coincides with the calculations of Shri Bansal and those in the text of Surya-Siddhant.

Therefore, it can be said that Mahabharata war took place nearly five thousand years from now. There are various other evidences and details, but we leave them here, for the sake of brevity.

Some people, such as Max Muller and others have had trouble accepting this date as the time of Mahabharata, because they felt that the descriptions of the planetary positions of the Saptrishi (Ursa Major) were not real. However a similar description is also given in the second chapter of the twelfth canto of the Bhagvata Purana, which helps verify the time of Mahabharata.

However, this is yet another example of the bias, of most of the western scholars against the Indian culture and heritage and down playing it without verifying the facts.

The scientists have developed so many software packages like (1) Planetarium, (2) Ecliptic, (3) Lode-Star and (4) Punching for determination of ancient events with unthinkable accuracy.

The different scholars have arrived at almost the same dates, of course with some variations in their calculations, which are quite natural, but it confirms and not impairs the historicity of Krishna and Mahabharata.

Thus, India's most beloved dignitary Bhagwan Krishna was a genuinely historical figure who walked this planet about 5000 years ago, lived around the time of 3200-3100 B.C., and for 126 years of age, approximately.

(Data based on various resources and the studies)